SHIFT

The true story of how my whole life changed and
I discovered the joy of living

Mudita

BALBOA
PRESS

A DIVISION OF HAY HOUSE

Balboa Press books may be ordered through booksellers or by contacting:

Balboa Press
A Division of Hay House
1663 Liberty Drive
Bloomington, IN 47403
www.balboapress.com
1-(877) 407-4847

ISBN: 978-1-4525-6505-7 (sc)
ISBN: 978-1-4525-6506-4 (e)

Balboa Press rev. date: 12/18/2012

I would like to acknowledge and thank my parents for raising me in freedom and Sue, Heather, Jo, Sarah, Daphne, Steve and the team of Balboa Press for helping me with this book!

Preface

*T*his is my personal story. It is a story of change during times where change is appearing in many people's lives and on our whole planet. There is a shift in consciousness happening that will get us to a different place to live our lives from.

I believe that this shift isn't suddenly occurring in 2012 but has started to take place some years ago and will continue to do so in the coming years.

I didn't write this book because I think that my story is something special. I wrote this book to share my experience and encourage others to dare to follow their heart and live their highest dreams, even if it means moving through stages of uncertainty and fear.

I wrote this book in English to reach a wider audience. I apologize if my English sounds sometimes 'a little weird' to you, as it isn't my first language.

By now, I've told my story to many people and friends. Some of them have felt inspired to change their lives too. They too have taken the risk and stepped out of their either boring or too demanding life routine. They too have felt a little wobbly at times but are now living a life that is more an expression of what's right and true for them.

Many of us are used to creating a lot of unhappiness and complications in our lives. Why not create happiness for a change?

*   *   *

Prologue

A golden sun is rising behind the kowhai tree and as I'm watching it through my bedroom window, I feel amazed how my whole life has changed by my own choice.

"When life is nice, is there any reason for change?" one might wonder.

I find if we want to grow and develop—yes! If we want to expand our life, we need to leave what is well known and step out into the unknown. There are infinite possibilities for us to be, to experience, to find and to express ourselves. It never gets boring when we live, constantly opening up to more . . .

Healing

*I*t all began in Greece in the year 2000 when I suddenly felt "I can't breathe".

My partner and I had just moved into our newly built house when I felt "I cannot breathe".

What was wrong? I should be happy. I had been dreaming about this house for many years. When my mother sold my grandfather's house, she gave me the money to buy a piece of land. After a long search, I found this olive grove on the hillside with a marvellous sea and sunset view. What followed was the whole process of planning and building the house and waiting for the day we could finally move in.

All my hopes for happiness were built into this house that truly had become very beautiful. Now, all it was to me was a golden cage. I remembered a song my partner had put on during our first night together: "White bird in a golden cage" and I realized, the cage was truly golden but it still felt like a cage! It wouldn't let me be free. Or was it that next to my partner I didn't feel free and the house that should be a nest had become a cage to me?

The signs had been there. I just had been so busy with the whole process of building the house that I had ignored them. First my lovely teenage daughter had left. She didn't want to live any longer under the same roof with my partner.

Then the dogs left. They kept running away and when they discovered how much fun it was to hunt one

1

of the villager's sheep, we had to either shoot or give them away.

It was on my birthday when I made the decision to leave too. The man I was with was too dominating, overpowering and controlling. I felt myself expanding, while he tried to keep me small and under his control. Our relationship felt like a shoe that doesn't fit any longer. So I left the man, the house and the countryside where I had lived for 12 years and went to town.

At that stage, I felt very attracted to a man from New Zealand who lived in Greece, not to say I had fallen in love with him. I started dreaming about going to New Zealand with him and really could see myself living there. That was not a real option though. Apart from the fact that I wouldn't move so far away from my child, he wasn't interested in me.

I still allowed myself to indulge in my own fantasies and desires and as I suffered, one of my friends asked me: "What is it that you like about him?"

"Oh", I answered "he is spiritual . . . he is a healer . . . he lives consciously . . . and he has also got a strong sexual aura!"

She said: "So these are the qualities you long to have in your life. Try to see it this way: look passed the man and see what he embodies. This is what you want!"

I had been on a spiritual path and working as a holistic massage therapist for years but I wanted a man to share the path with me. I was dreaming of meditating together, massaging each other and making love consciously. I saw all this happening in a house in the countryside in front of a fireplace.

Instead my reality looked totally different. I moved into an apartment in town that was surrounded by other apartment blocks, traffic noise and loud living neighbours. After all those years living in a stone house in nature, (first an old rented one, then my own new one) with the view of stunning sunsets above the sea and the sounds of bees and birds and barking dogs, the change was immense! Funnily enough, I liked it because it was so different, and I had never experienced living like this before.

I was glad my daughter came and lived with me again. Things weren't easy though. She was still very angry with me that I had forced her to live with a man she didn't like and that I didn't tell him to move out when she couldn't take it anymore. She was so angry she wouldn't listen to anything I said. She also refused to eat the food I cooked for us. I tried hard to heal the past with love and care but all I received from her was anger and rejection.

So instead of living with a man who loved me, I was living with a daughter who hated me, and my love and wish to care for her turned into helplessness and desperation.

When things fall apart and in times of difficulty we are lucky to have friends—and friends I had many!

When I left my house and before I got my apartment, my friends opened their doors for me, let me stay in their homes, took their time to talk to me and with the help of their love and support, I got through those hard times until things became better.

When we are not sure exactly where we are going, it is good to move forward in small steps. In moments, when I felt too shaky to take *any* step, I sat down on the earth, feeling the earth under me. Where ever I was and where ever I would go, the earth would always be there and carry me. The sky would always be above me and inspire me. The earth would always carry me. People might come and go—the earth would always be there. Feeling the connection with the earth gave me peace.

In town, I made new contacts, and as a massage therapist I started to work with a different sort of client: musicians, actors and dancers. The more subtle and sensitive my clients were, the more they liked my work and the better I could relate to them. One of Greece's star actresses even wanted to employ me as her personal massage therapist but she was based in Athens and I, being a mother, couldn't just move there. The success of my work though, was good for me during this stage of transition. It healed and nurtured my self-confidence that had suffered in my last partnership.

It happened that one of my friends had just done a course in hypnotherapy and needed to practice a form of timeline therapy that takes two continuous days of wiping out past trauma conditions, which block us today. I was grateful to be one of her guinea pigs and to get the chance for a general, major clearing process, that would further support me, by letting me have a sort of "fresh start".

I also used affirmations to attract beautiful experiences and people into my life. After a year I attracted a new partner who, I thought, was the best man in town (and I still think he is!). He was an adventurous, playful, inspired and free spirit, living his visions.

I also felt a need for expansion in the field of my therapeutic work. I started training in CranioSacral Therapy and that was the start of a journey into new dimensions of the healing work. The training contained and was based on self-experience and became a further process of my own healing and transformation. Apart from techniques, I learned how to connect with the body's innate healing force and to communicate with the body consciousness. I learned how to communicate with my own all-knowing body consciousness and let it teach me what is true for me, and what I need to know in order to be balanced in my life. I felt blessed to witness the healing change and grow, in the people I worked with. In fact I witnessed "unbelievable" body processes occur in others and was absolutely amazed by the power of the body's innate healing force. Healing and transformation had become my new passion.

This journey has no end—"once on the path, always on the path!" some people say—but as we go along life becomes easier and lighter.

I had got "on the path" quite early. In High School my friends and I started experimenting with soft drugs. After being "high" I got to experience how it is to go really "low" and often felt so depressed that I could hardly handle it. My own father, who was a psychologist and body worker, made me aware of what was going on in my psyche and showed me ways to work with it. Since then, I had been reading many books on self-help and analysing myself.

Now, I seemed to move through a phase of my life where self-healing had become essential.

I participated in workshops of Family Constellation Therapy that takes healing to the level of our whole family system and as this work can be taken further to look at any relationship dynamics, I looked at the situation around my house. My ex-partner was still living there and I was considering buying him out. The constellation showed me moving away from the house into a happy future.

Funnily enough my efforts at first went in the opposite direction! I tried hard to find a solution to keep the house. None of my attempts had any success and after a while, I finally decided to sell the house. Selling the house turned out to be so easy, I would never have imagined it! It felt like the universe was supporting this solution (as the constellation had already shown).

To me personally though, it wasn't so easy to let go of the house I had created, the house I had dreamed about for many years. It cost me many tears but when I finally signed the papers to sell, I felt so free!

I had lost my nest but I had gained wings to fly! The money I had now, opened up new possibilities. I took my daughter on a trip to India and our relationship started to heal.

When some of my clients, who knew that I practiced yoga, asked me repeatedly whether I could teach them, I started to study yoga. Another journey began, on which I found my spiritual family, but that's another story.

I made new dreams. One of the dreams I had, since I was a teenager, was to live in a village with my friends, where everyone has their own personal space and freedom and where we can come together and work together as we wish to.

My new partner had a piece of land and together we made an attempt to form such a village with some of our friends. Everyone enjoyed dreaming about it, but when it came to get involved financially no one went a step further. My partner and I changed the dream. We thought of creating an alternative tourist village. That could be the project to keep us busy for the rest of our lives. In the meantime we were running a small cafe that became a venue for live-music events. We were also running a large open-air theatre that hosted major events; not only theatre plays but concerts as well. The whole process of realizing my partner's visions was an adventure in itself, with many exciting, high-energy moments and artistic highlights. We also made a plan for marriage. Everything went really well. I had come to a really good point in my life and my career when I suddenly felt my whole life shifting again! . . .

*   *   *

The Call

Some time ago, one of my friends had organized a seminar with Greta, a lady from Vienna who channels messages for us from "spirit", which is really the divine self in each one of us, our own spiritual dimension. The messages tell us, who we really are and what we need to know. She often combines her work with trips into different countries as that provides for people time and space to exploring themselves in a different environment, in a new territory.

When she was going with a group of people to New Zealand, I could hardly think about anything else. My mind kept circling around that fact and I just felt, I had to go too!

Still I wasn't sure. "Such a big trip . . . expensive too . . . .", I was thinking. My logical mind didn't know how to deal with the situation. It was my intuitive mind that kept pushing though. As I sat down in meditation and relaxed, I felt my soul calling me to New Zealand. When I thought about all the plans, I had made with my partner in Greece, the marriage, the alternative tourist project, it suddenly felt all wrong and heavy. Within a glimpse of a moment, I saw a life-circle coming to an end for me in Greece.

I once had agreed with my first Greek husband that our daughter would grow up in Greece. At that time, I wanted to travel around the world. As we were traveling together through Israel and Egypt, I found out that I was pregnant and we decided to have the child, go back to

Greece and marry. (Our marriage didn't last long though.) Now, she'd grown up and had moved abroad to study there. So that mission was fulfilled. Practically I was now free to go anywhere.

And—yes—I felt ready for something new!

Still, I was scared to my bones to face the truth that I just had seen. I loved my Greek partner and was happy with him. The idea of moving on and moving away from him made me sad. I was comfortable where I was and with my work I was more successful then ever before.

"Do I really have to start all over again?", I thought.

"Wait" I calmed myself down, "You are only thinking about a holiday right now." Lying to myself didn't make me feel any better.

I asked for a message from "above" what that urge to leave for New Zealand was all about. The answer was surprising. I got a message about finding my soul mate there.

Since I was young, the idea that we have a soul mate had always felt so true and uplifting to me. I thought that there must be a person for everyone of us that just fits to our psycho-biological structure; like two pieces of a puzzle fit into each other.

"Is there really a man for me in New Zealand?" I kept wondering. I remembered the New Zealander to whom I had felt so attracted to some years ago. Had I felt like this because something inside me knew that the man of my destiny is a New Zealander? That was exciting!

The excitement left me soon though, and fear got hold of me again.

This sudden urge to leave for New Zealand was still confusing. I had seen a glimpse of the truth while I was in meditation. In my daily life though I was functioning with my logical mind, which didn't understand it, nor did it know what to do with it. Doubts came up. I longed for more clarity.

At this stage, it happened that my craniosacral therapy teachers were giving an encounter-seminar on the next coming weekend at Mount Pelion. Encounter here, meant encounter with oneself!

I thought that this might help me to find some answers on a deeper level of myself. I hoped to gain a better understanding of my drives and my fears and I decided to go.

Due to my mental state, the drive to Mount Pelion from Southern Greece seemed very, very long to me. The fact that it was winter and the weather was cold and rainy wasn't helpful either.

To make it a little easier, I stopped over in Athens where one of my friends had an apartment. She herself wasn't there, but had given me the keys to it. It was quiet late when I arrived. The place was all empty, dark and cold. Feeling alone and vulnerable, I fell into a sleep that didn't last long. When I woke up a few hours later, the silence felt heavy on my chest. It was only 4.30 in the morning and I started the journey into a deep dark, cold and rainy day.

I felt the darkness coming over me like a shroud, creeping into my soul and felt reminded of what is called, "The dark night of soul". The trip felt endless. So did the darkness!

Then finally after hours, the daylight broke through but as the weather was bad, the blackness only changed into greyness. How unusual for Greece! Or was it just reflecting me?

*   *   *

A small group had come together for the workshop. The welcome is always warm and loving with lots of hugging and soon I felt better. Here, I could be myself and didn't need to pretend anything. Here, we all share

9

our thoughts, feelings and emotions without judgment and if one of us is falling, the others will be there to hold him/her.

As I was sharing my confusion around that inner call to New Zealand, I realized that this meant also saying goodbye to this group and to my teachers. We had been together for a number of years, during the training and additional seminars, and we had seen each other going through all kind of physical and emotional processes. They were like a family to me. It became clear though, that this was going to happen, I would have to say goodbye to them.

Funnily enough, one of the issues we worked on during this seminar was cutting the psychological umbilical cord to the mother. Most of us think of ourselves as being independent adults but are we really? How many of us feel like we can't live without our partner, husband or wife? That is still the child in us.

We also worked around our needs. How do we feel, when they are met and how do we feel, when they are not met in our relationships? I channelled the energy of both. First, I felt myself blossom then fading just like a flower, dependent on if it is watered or not.

My need was to be loved in depth, to devote and open myself fully, allowing myself to be touched deep inside. I realized how I missed that in my present partnership.

My partner loved me but he was always in a hurry. So we rarely met on a deeper level. As if he was afraid of that, he often kept it superficial. He also was very occupied with his own needs, usually not asking about mine. We were kind of both busy, looking after his needs.

Looking at it like this, made it a little easier for me to open up to something new, to something different.

I remembered a dream that I had two years ago, when I had to deal with a health issue. In this dream the doctor had written out the prescription; a journey to the most beautiful places on earth!

Would my journey also be part of an inner healing process?

*   *   *

Following my heart

*T*wo weeks later, I called my teachers from the airport. They weren't at home. So I left a message on their answer machine, just to let them know that I was finally going. I heard my own voice sounding fragile and my knees felt kind of wobbly. However, there I was, ready to board an airplane to the other side of the earth.

I had the itinerary from Greta's group, though no one knew that I was coming. When I finally made my decision, they had already left Austria. The plane reached Dubai at 11pm and—how nice—I was brought to a hotel, where I could have a proper sleep. My onward flight wasn't departing until at 10.30 in the morning. I could even have a leisurely breakfast at the hotel buffet, all paid for by the airline. Next stop over was in Australia, for just one hour and here I got the chance to buy myself a travel guide. In the Greek town where I lived, no bookstore had a travel guide for New Zealand. So I had three hours left to find out as much as I could about the country I was visiting, before my plane landed there.

When I first saw Aotearoa (as it is called by the Maori, I now knew) from the airplane, I was surprised to see lots of brown hills. That wasn't how I had imagined it! The inner picture I had was full of green and freshness.

"Let's see what else might be totally different about this country from what I imagine", I thought.

A look on the map showed that Christchurch, where I was going to land, is in the South Island.

My God, I hadn't even been aware that the country consists of two islands. A look on the itinerary showed the group was in Dunedin. I was wondering, whether I should try to go there straight away or stay in Christchurch and get some sleep. On the 20 hours flight from Dubai, I hadn't been able to sleep at all. When I went to the information desk in the airport, I found out that soon there would be a bus leaving for Dunedin.

"How long does it take to get there?" I asked.

"Six hours", the lady at the desk answered. I felt too excited to sleep anyway, and I could fall asleep on the bus if I needed to.

"One ticket, please" I heard myself saying.

I was told that the bus would leave in about an hour just outside the terminal.

"*About* an hour" I was wondering. "Don't they have a fixed time table in this country?" I went over to the public phone to call home and say that I had arrived safely. As I was approaching the phone, a couple of young travellers asked me if I wanted their phone card. They were leaving and the card was nearly full.

"Great, thank you!"

"What a good start!" I thought. Then I realized it was two o'clock in the afternoon, which meant middle of the night in Europe. "Whom was I going to call at this time . . . ?"

I stepped outside into a fresh breeze. The sun was out but the wind was quite cold. It was the beginning of March and early autumn over here.

"The wind is coming right from the South Pole." I was told. Only a handful of people were waiting for the bus that seemed to take its time to pick us up. At least I got two seats to myself and so I had the chance to stretch out my legs, while we were driving through a flat agricultural area southward. The bus driver had the radio on and they were playing a lot of old rock songs. That was very different from what I was used to! In Greece the bus drivers drive me mad with their music. As I was listening to a song from Pink Floyd, I was wondering whether I fitted into this country better . . .

*   *   *

When I arrived at the hostel where Greta and the group were staying, I was lucky to get a bed in a dorm.

"We have just one bed left because there is a group from Austria staying here, at the moment," the young woman in the reception said.

"Yes, I know" I answered, "that's why I'm here. I wanted to catch up with them." "Oh, it's a good time for that. They are just having their dinner."

They were surprised when I suddenly showed up. "Hadn't Greta/Spirit said we should be ready for surprises, on her last channelling in Athens?" I remembered.

Only Greta and her manager Barbara knew me. The rest of the group were Austrians that I had never met. They all welcomed me and were more or less nice to me, the stranger that had so suddenly appeared amongst them. I felt overwhelmed by the group energy. My chest felt contracted, and when I mentioned it to Greta, she sensed an energy at my solar plexus that was pulling me away.

After the meeting, I was glad to retreat to my room and let myself fall into the bed. Sleep, sleep, sleep was all I wanted. When I woke up, it was three o'clock in the morning. I felt wide-awake.

The next time I woke up, it was nearly ten. The group had already had their breakfast and their morning circle. They were ready to start a tour to the steepest street of the world and the Otago Peninsula. Quickly, I had some breakfast and joined them.

*   *   *

Next to Greta I felt wonderfully light and free. Through her, "spirit" was telling us that it is our choice to live in freedom and allowance of joy and wellbeing. So many of us have a deep rooted feeling of not deserving a good and joyful life. To many of us it feels "righter" to have problems that need to be solved and happiness is something we hope for at some point in the far future. When I spoke to her about the calling that I felt into something new—a new life, a new partner, New Zealand—she tuned in and saw me step-by-step bringing things to an end in Greece. She/Spirit said that I wouldn't need to start all over again. Instead I was already living my new life!

She/Spirit also said that I basically don't need anyone else, as I'm complete and happy in myself. In my case though, marriage seems to be the right thing. As she was saying this, I saw a piece of land with a wooden house in a garden. I looked at it from a downhill perspective. The vision was brief but it left a nice and warm feeling about my destiny with me.

When I sensed feelings of guilt about leaving so many people behind (my partner, all my clients and yoga students), the answer from Greta/ Spirit was very clear: It is all about taking the FULL responsibility for ourselves. We are responsible only for ourselves and our own life and what everybody else does with our decisions is their thing.

I needed to get used to the idea. I still felt somehow responsible for the wellbeing of others in a way that I often took on other people's burdens, issues and symptoms, in order to help or heal them. But it was true; we can't carry a cross for other people! They carry it for a reason and trying to help them carry it also means that we don't consider them capable of carry it themselves.

When the jet lag left me and I felt that I had fully arrived, I started massaging members of the group. They loved to have the opportunity to have a massage while they were traveling and I enjoyed it too. "Spirit" confirmed that it was good for me to do a little bit of my work because it connected me with my heart.

One of the people I massaged was a well-known osteopath. He told me how he had worked in foreign countries and gave me some good advise on how to set myself up. He said that with my hands I could work everywhere in the world and I felt encouraged.

During the following days, we had many magical experiences. We walked along a beach at low tide to a large cave where we spontaneously joined our voices and filled the space with beautiful sounds.

We did a bush walk through New Zealand's magnificent native forest to a waterfall that seemed pretty spectacular to me, at the time. Later, I became aware that was just normal here in New Zealand. Ferns were growing like palm trees here and I felt amazed by all the lushness. That was more like the inner picture I had of New Zealand. There was all the green freshness I had longed for. My heart filled with joy. When everyone else was gone, I still stood by the waterfall, singing and greeting the divine mother in nature.

We saw the flight of an albatross, we encountered seals, sea lions and penguins.

My highlight was being in the ocean with dolphins. I had been dreaming about it for years. To my great disappointment the group had already been swimming with dolphins before my arrival. Then, it got even better than I had expected: on our tour through the Caitlins we reached a long bay with a cafe close to the beach. On a sign it said that a family of more than 20 hector dolphins lived there. Close by was a telescope and when I looked I could hardly believed what I saw. There was someone with a wetsuit in the water and dolphins were swimming around that person.'

"Here is my chance", I thought, not caring about the cloudy, windy and rainy weather. Full of excitement I ran down the beach to where the dolphins were. I had no swimsuit or towel with me. My one-piece underwear would do as a swimsuit, I decided, and entered the water. The water was cold but I was far too excited to pay any attention to it. The woman swimming with the dolphins was splashing the surface of the water with her hands, which seemed to attract them. I copied her and had the idea of making some sound into the water. Suddenly, I saw a fin coming towards me. Playfully the dolphin swam once around me and then it was gone with the next wave. Then it came back. By now some other people had entered the water. The dolphins kept swimming from one person to another and all around us. Never before, had I seen such small dolphins. Hector dolphins are only about a meter long. They are the smallest on earth. I felt their playful, joyful spirit with me even after the dolphins had left.

The two young guys from Israel, who had been in the water not far from me, seemed to be very joyful too. They were laughing a lot as they were looking at me and now I realized what else they were joyful about. When I looked down at my body I saw that my white underwear had turned see-through and I was practically naked standing there.

"Never mind" I thought. I had been swimming with dolphins!

*   *   *

Later on that day, during the evening circle, we received more beautiful messages from Spirit. Most of us had encountered the dolphins and had felt the same heart opening, euphoric effect.

Spirit told us: "It is your choice to have a magnificent life. Everything old that doesn't allow that, just breathe it out!"

Spirit also talked about psychic people, picking up constantly on other people's thoughts and emotions and therefore needing to spend time alone. I was one of these cases.

"You all are psychic and you only need a channel until you develop this ability yourself."

There were some more personal messages for me. I heard that one of my legs hadn't psychically fully developed and was now receiving new energy. I was told that due to that shift in my lower body there could be a change in my pelvic area.

One lady wanted to understand what didn't work in her life. Spirit said "Heaven laughs when you say: I have to understand it first, then I can let it go. You just have to be willing to let it go. Change is happening beyond all understanding!"

That stuck with me! I liked it! Hadn't I too been analysing all my life-situations in order to free myself from suffering, always wanting to understand everything?

Three deep breaths, breathing out everything heavy, was much easier and it worked on the spot. How great was that?

"Now take a fresh new breath! Every breath is new and you can be new too, with each new breath."

How cool was that? I loved it!

* * *

In Queenstown by Lake Wakatipu I left the group. It felt totally wrong to me to travel through New Zealand with a group of Austrians. I felt the need to get to know "Kiwis", as New Zealanders are often called. They seemed to be laid back and humorous people.

Before I left, Greta/Spirit had said that by going my own path in freedom I was doing something for the whole group. They would all benefit from it.

So I decided from now on to follow my heart on my own discovery tour. Tuning in into the energy of "now" I felt my needs or got a sudden idea what step to take next.

First of all I needed to become still. First the long journey from Greece—and since my arrival here I had been constantly on the move.

I had heard about a lodge at the other end of Lake Wakatipu, secluded from town and neighbours, and as my heart jumped by the thought of it, I decided to go there and have some quiet time.

Leaving the shelter of the group behind me, I walked down the road, pulling the suitcase on wheels with me. The group had hired their own bus and driver what made traveling easy and comfortable. Now, I had to see how I would find my way around and as public transport was bad in this area, I decided to hitchhike. In the eighties, it was still common to hitchhike but nowadays no one seemed to do it anymore in Europe. However it still seemed to be quite common in this country and it didn't take long for me to get a ride to the other end of the lake.

The owner of the lodge picked me up at the nearest dairy and Information Centre, all in one. His little son was with him and on our thirty minutes drive he kept on talking to his dad.

"Excuse me dad . . ." was how he started every sentence and I was pretty impressed by so much politeness between a father and a small child. Again that was very different to what I was used to.

The place where I was taken to was truly quiet and peaceful. After checking, in I walked down to the lake.

Happily, I found a beautiful spot by the waterfront to sit down and relax. Taking in the scenery and the sounds of nature was all I wanted—but ouch—what was that? Small black flies covered my arms and legs and they were biting me! How could I relax like this? They were not leaving me alone!

"Sandflies!", I was told in the hostel. Hadn't I heard about them? They seemed to be the little devils in paradise. I escaped inside.

There were many brochures and flyers about what to do in the area. I picked one about horse riding. Yes—that sounded adventurous: discovering the valley on the back of a horse. I went to book a tour at the reception of the lodge. The problem was, how would I get to the stables?

A pick-up from the hostel would put another 30 dollars on the tour that was quite pricy anyway.

Where was the line between being willing to pay for the experience and staying inside my budget?

"Hey" said the young German receptionist "you can take our car."

Thanks to the friendly couple who worked in the lodge—her partner was the cook there—I found myself driving along the dirt road the next day, feeling slightly nervous while I was trying to stay on the left side of the road. The fact that I hadn't done much riding since my childhood, added some more excitement to it.

"Didn't you want to just have some quiet time?", a voice inside me asked. "How boring when there is so much more to discover and experience!", another voice answered. Amused I listened to my own inner dialogue.

The horses were well trained and it was easy to ride them. Some of them had been used for the filming the Lord Of The Rings. Wow—I thought I had seen the scenery somewhere before. So that was where I had seen it: in the movie.

Several times we crossed the river and disturbed a couple of "paradise" ducks. The horses seemed to enjoy it. They were splashing water all over my legs as they went along. Later, we cantered up the hill and got to a spot from where we had a magnificent view over "Paradise—as it was really called—and a majestic mountain range.

How could someone stay inside and read a book when there was so much magnificence to experience?

The next day, I finally took it easy though and did some reading and journaling in the morning.

I met some other tourists and was told about the amazingly beautiful Milford Sound. Someone else was excited about skydiving. It was good talking to them and getting some ideas about what the options and possibilities were.

For now, I was satisfied with a leisurely walk along the lake and into the bush. I sat down on the forest ground and listened to the birds, forgetting about myself and everything else. When the sun disappeared behind the hill and the air chilled down, I walked back. A little further, the sun was still throwing a golden light on the hillside. The air was filled with blown up dandelions that were drifting along in a cosmic dance.

Back at the lodge three more people had moved inside my room. They too had been on an adventurous trip: three days on a track through the mountain range. They looked quite exhausted but their eyes were shiny. One of the guys started a conversation with me. His name was Jason and he was from Wellington. As we were talking, I felt a nice connection and attraction between us. We were inspiring each other and got totally involved in the conversation until his girlfriend, who had come over from America for a visit, pulled him away.

The same night I heard him sighing in his bed and felt strangely touched by it. I listened to him breathing, which was weird and just wanted to lie down next to him, which was even weirder!

The next morning we were all leaving. They were in a hurry to make it for the boat that would take them across the lake and we quickly said goodbye. It didn't feel right though. It felt like something was missing here. Then, I met Jason again as he was waiting outside. This time he was alone. He gave me his phone number, and offered to show me the best place for a good coffee in Wellington, when I would pass through there. Something inside me went: "Yes!" I have to admit, I wanted to see him again.

*   *   *

There was no choice where to go next. The road led back to Queenstown, the party-town of the south, home of bungy jumping and all kinds of adventure sports.

When I first heard about bungy jumping, it seemed to me the craziest thing to do. Now, I thought it would be a good test as to whether I could develop enough trust to overcome the fear. One of the girls in my room was crying because she had booked a bungy jump the day before and was now so scared. Soon she would be picked up by a bus to take her to the bridge. That didn't encourage me much. I felt kind of sensitive at that moment and decided to take the gondola up to the hilltop do something less challenging instead. On the "Luge" one could ride a three-wheeled cart down a 'scenic' track first before getting on a more advanced track with sharp bends and tunnels in it. That was fun and easy enough for kids to do. There even was a small bungy area where I could watch others letting themselves fall over the edge. That was fun too, watching their faces before the fall.

My stomach turned when the gondola started to take me downhill and I laughed about myself even considering a bungy jump.

Back in the hostel, I saw a note on the board saying that someone was offering a lift up to Wellington for shared petrol costs. I wanted to get to Kaikoura that was on the way and we agreed to travel together the next day. Until then, what else was possible?

"Live music tonight" it said at the Irish Pub. When I entered there weren't many people inside. The music wasn't Irish at all, as I had expected it to be. Still I enjoyed listening while sipping on my beer. A nice looking guy was standing all by himself at a table on the other side of the Pub and after a while he invited me to come over. "Should I? Why not?" I asked myself.

I'm glad I did because we had a nice communication going on between us. He was a hang gliding teacher from Sweden, working here during the tourist season. He invited me to fly with him the next day and I would have loved to, if I hadn't already arranged the trip up to Kaikoura. We spend a beautiful evening together and hugged each other goodbye, before I returned into my hostel.

*　　*　　*

In the followings days, I met many nice people, some on the road, some in hostels. When our heart is open, friends are everywhere. Travellers often are open and communicate easily with each other. That's a wonderful experience. Most of the backpackers were in their early twenties. I had my 42nd birthday on this trip and thought that my psychological age was probably 24. I liked that the new year of my life started in New Zealand and wondered if this could be an omen for where the next year would take me. I shared my birthday cake with friends I had just made. Some of them I would meet again and others not. It didn't matter. It was the moment when we shared a certain experience that counted. Afterwards, we all continued our own journey in freedom.

I hiked through the Abel Tasman National Park with its golden beaches and rich native forests. I reached Golden Bay where many artists, hippies and people who look for an alternative life style have settled. That's where I discovered "a place for me": Shambhala.

I'd describe it as an "alternative" backpacker's hostel with solar power, composting toilets and a large meditation hall. The owner had created lots of artistic little corners and the property went right down to the sea. It just had everything I like and I instantly felt at home there. I would have liked to spend the rest of my life there but right now there was much more to discover and I left after three nights.

"Oh, you're already leaving", the owner said when I said good-bye.

"Yes, this time I haven't got much time but next time I would like to stay longer and work as a "wwoofer" (willing worker for food and accommodation)."

"OK," he said.

"OK", I confirmed and so simply it was settled. By then I knew already that I wanted to come back to New Zealand. One month was just not enough to see the whole country.

When I reached Wellington after a windy ferry ride, I phoned Jason who wanted to take me for coffee. He offered me a spare room in his house where I could stay. Gratefully I accepted and started to feel excited. How would it be to see him again? I remembered how I had felt that night in the hostel.

To get to his place, I had to take another ferry. When he picked me up, we were both glad, that the conversation flowed as easily as before and there was no taste of embarrassment. We once again seemed to inspire each other and this created a pleasant enthusiasm between us. At the same time, there was an ease and trust between us. Soon we talked about our personal life, our love life and relationships. I learned that the woman, who had been with him when we first met, was an old friend from university. They weren't a couple, as I had guessed. I told him about my partner in Greece and how I had suddenly felt this pulling and calling to New Zealand.

During the first night I spent there, I felt like a fire had been lit inside me. It didn't let me get much sleep. What had I been thinking? The signs had been already there when we had stayed in the same room in the hostel and I had listened to his breath.

The next morning, he admitted that he hadn't had much sleep either. We couldn't help ourselves; the attraction was too strong and finally overwhelmed us.

I had sensations of fire in my body like I had never felt before. Was that part of the change in my lower body as Greta had foreseen it? Or was it due to him that I felt like that? Was he the man of my destiny?

Days passed quickly. He was working during the daytime while I went to the museum Te Papa, to the botanic gardens and the National Gallery. I even got to listen to the prime minister, debating, during a tour in parliament.

I felt sad when I left. I felt, I had fallen in love but how was he feeling? I wasn't sure. He knew, I had a partner in Greece and made no attempt to keep me with him. And my own journey didn't end there. There was still more to discover!

On Jason's recommendation, I took the "Overlander", which is a very slow train, traveling between Wellington and Auckland, to get to the volcanic region at National

Park. If one is willing to give it the time one is rewarded with a magnificent scenery!

When I got off the train at National Park, it was surprisingly cold there. I waited inside the station for my pick-up to the hostel that I had booked beforehand. I would definitely need to put some warmer clothes on!

Once I had checked in and dressed with a woollen jersey and a raincoat I was keen to get on one of the shorter tracks. I hitchhiked and it didn't take long to get a lift to the entrance of the nearest park. I recognized the landscape from "Lord of the Rings" and soon felt like I was in the middle of a fairy tale. The weather was misty too and I didn't meet a single person on the track that I had chosen. There is something truly magical about the volcanic grounds. I was fascinated by it as I slowly wandered along in a zone of "no time".

Forced by hard rain I finally returned to the hostel, filled with peace, and I was happy to just relax for the rest of the day. The next day I needed to get up early for a one-day excursion through the volcanoes that is known as "Tongariro Crossing" and supposed to be NZ's most spectacular day trip. To my disappointment the tour was cancelled due to bad weather conditions. That is one thing about New Zealand: many outdoor activities just depend on the weather.

In Taupo, I felt brave enough to go for skydiving but once again it was cancelled because of bad weather. Instead I walked along the river and found some hot springs. That was just the right thing: lying in the warm water by the river as the raindrops fell on top of me. When I returned to town I saw the platform for bungy jumping. I went closer and looked at the beautiful deep green river below. It looked wide and deep. This was a spot where I could imagine to letting myself fall. The water below didn't scare me. Another good thing was that I didn't need to make any booking. I could just walk there. I felt positive about giving it a go and I did so the next morning.

Telling all my body cells that we are not going to die though it may look like it and singing out loud, I walked along the road out of town to the office and from there straight onto the platform, not giving myself any time to think. My heart was pumping wildly though and I was breathing heavily while the bungy was fixed around my ankles. The employee who did it asked me a lot of questions to distract my mind. I must have looked quite stressed. Then I was given a short demonstration how to keep my back straight and do the "free fall" on the count of three.

In small steps, as my feet were tied together, I walked towards the edge. Not being able to move my feet freely felt horrible. Then I was told to look up into the camera to get my photo taken. That was a good trick to avoid me staring straight into the gap. I heard them counting down for me and, bringing up all the trust I had somewhere inside me, I let myself fall.

The video later showed that I was gone by the count of two. Someone said it looked elegant. It *felt* totally crazy though! The whole body system gets the information of "danger: catastrophe!". There is nothing joyful about it! I heard funny sounds coming out of my mouth as I, while hanging from my feet, was bouncing up and down. Soon it was all over and I was pulled into a boat and brought to shore. My back hurt. I must have pulled a muscle as my arms were swinging around while I was hanging and bouncing. I felt my blood rushing through my head and body so fast that could not think. All I felt, was a wave of euphoria hitting me and such a boost of energy kicking in that I *ran* uphill back to the office. I felt so amazingly strong and proud that I raised my fist like a winner: "I did it . . . . I did it . . . I did it!!!"

In the office they were now showing my video. When I watched my bungy jump on the large screen I really felt like a hero. I had succeeded and felt the victory of overcoming my fears with trust.

There is something about a bungy jump that, apart from the blissful high after the shock, empowers us. It gives us the gift of self-confidence. I now felt I could do anything!

One thing I couldn't do though after the bungy jump was sleep. The euphoria had stayed with me for the rest of the day and at night I was still full of energy. I wanted to go out and dance! Contagious as euphoria is, I made a whole group of backpackers come with me and we had so much fun that night, celebrating the beauty of an exciting life.

My time in New Zealand was slowly coming to an end. Only a few days were left until I would fly back to Greece. I had already extended my stay in NZ.

The last days of my journey I spent visiting more volcanic grounds, with steaming and bubbling pools of all kinds of colour and temperature. There I met the volcano in human form!

An elderly couple from Bavaria were on the same walkway with me. It was a warm and sunny day. They were traditionally dressed, course-buttoned up to the neck and the lady was sweating and puffing. She had difficulty walking, was slightly limping and proceeding slowly. While I was taking in the bubbling and steaming scenery from a park bench, I watched her turning into a path that had a sign warning people about the difficult grounds on the track. It said to proceed only if fitness is in good condition.

"Excuse me, I don't know how well you understand English. The sign says that this track is dangerous and to hike along there only in good physical condition", I said to her in an attempt to keep her safe.

She looked at me as if she couldn't believe what she just heard. Then she exploded, "What an insolence! How dare you? Mind your own business!" and I heard her grumbling, as she continued on the path. She was still grumbling when she reported to her husband what had happened.

When they came back together the husband made an unhappy face. I apologized to her, saying that I really didn't mean to offend her. "I just tried to be helpful", I tried to explain myself.

"I don't need your help!", she exploded again.

There was nothing more that I could say but "stay away from the steaming grounds" as the signs were saying.

In Rotorua with its eggy smell I took a single room to be by myself. I thought about Jason and my partner at home. My heart was in pain. I had played with the fire and burned myself.

I recovered my sore soul with an invigorating, bubbly mud bath at "Hell's Gate" and a pricy massage that was very average. The man in the reception said that I looked ten years younger when I returned to my room. A slight sulphuric smell still clung to me the next morning, when the shuttle bus took me from there straight to the airport.

My heart still felt troubled and I knew that wasn't because of leaving the country only. Jason was on my mind. I hadn't been able to leave him behind. I just hoped for good company on that very long flight back home. I also didn't feel quite sure if and for how much longer Greece would still be my home.

How heavenly was it arranged that I got to sit next to two other woman about my age who were both traveling on their own back to what once was their home.

On this very long flight, I found out that they were feeling troubled too. Sarah from London went there because her father was dying and Daniela went back to Serbia because her mother was dying. Compared to that my trouble seemed little.

We found out a lot more about each other on that trip and that we had a lot in common. They both offered for me to stay with them when I came back to New Zealand. No need to say that we became friends.

When our plane stopped over in Australia and we had to wait for an hour before getting back on board, one of us said, "I'm so glad you both are here with me. I had prayed for good company on this very long journey."

"Me too!"—"Me too!!" the others said in astonishment and this was the beginning of a sisterhood.

*   *   *

Bringing things to an end

When I landed in Athens, there was no one there to pick me up from the airport. My partner had a sore back and couldn't leave the house. I had to take the bus to get home, which added another 7 hours to the 33 hours long trip. The fact that on the day of my travel, I had woken up at 3 o'clock in the morning—because I was so excited before the trip—added up to 53 sleepless hours, when I finally arrived at home. Compared to the friendly, polite people and the often funny, humorous bus drivers in New Zealand, the Greeks suddenly seemed very rude to me.

I found my partner to be in much physical pain and mentally distressed by my absence. With a look full of blame he said, "Where have you been . . . ?"

On the day of my departure, we had been to a specialist for spinal conditions together. We both had been positive about a series of treatments he was going to receive there. I had expected him to be in good shape on my return, but one of the employees had done a wrong, exaggerated manipulation and he couldn't move since.

When he had told me about it, I hadn't been willing to finish my trip and come straight home to help him. I knew that other family members were there to help him, but that hadn't helped him psychologically. So in a way he was right to feel abandoned by me.

To make up for my *egoistic* behaviour, I spend the next days giving him extra care, while I tried to recover from the long journey and my jet lag.

Things weren't easy between us, as I couldn't spare him the truth that I was going to leave again. Since I didn't know how exactly my life would develop, I needed to cancel all our plans for the future and our marriage, which only added to his pain.

It hurt me to watch him suffer, but after getting to the bottom line of his pain, he decided to make the best out of the time we still had together. The whole process of my partner's crises was reflected in the events of the upcoming Easter celebration.

Easter is the biggest and most important religious celebration in Greece. The whole process of death and resurrection is practiced traditionally by a long fasting period. The fasting is broken at midnight of the Holy Saturday. During the service in the Orthodox Church, all the lights get switched off. Then the priest brings the new light in the form of a candle flame to the first waiting person. From there it spreads amongst all the people, who bring it into their homes. Then they break the fast with a special soup, the 'Mayiritsa'. The biggest feast of the year follows on Easter Sunday, when new life is greatly celebrated.

Parallel to this, something in our partnership had died too. We were celebrating a new status in our partnership by living the "here and now" of our being together, with an insecure future.

*   *   *

I also wanted to make the best out of my remaining time in Greece. In the healing circle with Greta and 'Spirit' I had learned to invite certain energies. The first one was always *light and love*. Another one—most unusual to many of us—was *the best*.

How many of us have learned to be content with *little* or just what we have got? As if we weren't worth having the best. By inviting *the best*, we were opening up to it and finally allowing ourselves to receive it.

The best for me in Greece included a house, where I could sit on a veranda and enjoy the sea and sunset view. I phoned a friend, who has a house in which she stays only during her summer holidays, and—yes—she was happy for me to be there the rest of the time. It was easy to reschedule my appointments and yoga classes, so I could have long weekends off work, and spend them there in the country.

The house was one of those old traditional stone houses and needed a deep general cleaning after the winter and everytime, when I first arrived there. But the rest of the time I could just enjoy.

After four days of work in town, I usually spent the first day just with myself. I loved the simplicity and the peace of the place for my own yoga and meditation practice. I had little and simple food and spent my time writing, studying some yoga scriptures and dreaming about my new life and a future that I couldn't see yet.

Sometimes I felt like my life was moving at high speed towards another shore, but I couldn't see the bridge yet.

"I move into perfect happiness" was my affirmation then, and I kept using it for a long time.

My partner spent some days with me in the old house in the country. After spending the first day in solitude, I usually was fine to socialize and see friends, or even give a treatment.

Every sunset became a ritual not to be missed. With the music of 'Sacred Spirit' and a glass of wine or *raki* I sat down on the veranda; some olives, tomatoes and feta cheese on the round, blue table in front of me.

In a dreaming state, I let my spirit fly over the sea and mountain ranges towards the setting sun. Each time was "the best"!

Looking at Venus which always follows the evening sun, my mind sometimes wandered to Jason in Wellington and these were not the only times, when it did so.

"Would I see him again? Would I stay with him again? What would it be like?" I was wondering.

I still wasn't sure about his feelings for me. I always felt a yes and a no coming from him. Was there any chance for it to become a yes?

I missed the star constellation of the Southern Cross on the stunning starlit night sky. Taking in all the beauty, I felt something was already pulling me away. That's why I was fully absorbing it.

I thought about the life I had in Greece that now seemed to come to an end. I had lived there for twenty years. I had always felt that it was part of my destiny to live there. Since I was a child, I had carried an inner picture of Greece in me, and wanted to go there.

I remembered, how the very first time I went on a holiday all by myself, I went to Greece and found it looking like the picture, I had carried inside me. At that time, I was only seventeen years old and still going to school.

Looking back, I remembered that each time when I came back from a holiday, I was suffering. I didn't like my own home country. It didn't feel at all like "home" to me. I had different dreams about living somewhere else.

Now, I remembered that another dream of mine had been to live in Australia or New Zealand.

At the age of seventeen, I read the book Siddharta by Herman Hesse and felt inspired to leave for India to sit by the Ganges River and to just meditate. There were many other countries that my adventurous spirit wanted to visit.

I remembered, how I made a plan to travel around the whole world, and stay and work in many different countries. I was fed up with school and learning from schoolbooks. I wanted to learn my lessons in life and let life teach me.

School at the same time was putting many demands on me. The final examinations were coming closer and my resistance to learning what I thought meaningless for my life, made it only worse. I had a boyfriend, at that stage, who shared my dream of traveling. He wanted to go on a trip around the world with me, but soon he broke up with me. I felt left alone by him and left alone with my dream.

The pain of the break-up on one hand and the pressure from school on the other hand became so much for me, that I nearly ended my life there. In fact I tried and survived through a miracle, but that is another story.

The lesson I learned from it was that I was supposed to live and that life was a gift that I would never waste again. I would finish school, and then I would find a way to live my dream and travel.

My plan was to go to the United States first, but here destiny came into play and worked its way. A dear friend, who at the time lived in the States, asked me whether I wanted to come to Greece with her. I had a good feeling about it, and decided I could start my trip from Greece. Then the friend moved without giving me her new address and never contacted me again. The outcome was, that I stuck to the new plan. I went to Greece first and that was, where love crossed my way. When I first met my husband, I had a feeling like I had known him forever.

I have already mentioned how my journey went as far as from Greece to Israel and Egypt, before my pregnancy took me to a crossing. I had to make a decision, where to go from here. I chose to go back to Greece with my boyfriend, marry and have the child. It hadn't been a logical decision. I had put the question inside me and the answer I had got was a clear yes; like that's where life wanted me to be. It had *felt right.*

I looked back at the years passed; the suffering I had endured during my marriage, and at the same time living in a place, that I loved and where I felt supported by the beauty and power of the land. During those first years in Greece, I went through the next school of learning the language, learning about the different mentality and how to deal with it. Hadn't I wanted to learn from life? Here I went, and it taught me many lessons.

Yes, twenty years in Greece had taught me a lot of beautiful things, I realized. I felt grateful for how it had shown me to go with the flow and let things develop. So often, when I had tried to make a fixed plan, I had heard, "We'll see!"

First of all, I had learned how to go slowly—'siga-siga'—and not rush things before they were ready.

Greek people came more from the heart than the head what had helped me to open my own heart and do what is often called "think with the heart".

In general, it was common to express emotions and I had often enjoyed to being able to shout at someone, when I felt angry. Everyone did it here. It was no big deal and one could still part as friends after shouting at each other.

I quite liked how rules where elastic and not rigid. "Here everything is forbidden and everything is allowed", I was often told. Of course that had another side to it and made it possible for a lot of corruption to take place. 'A little envelope' with money made many things possible, but beside this a *human* aspect would also be considered. For example, when a car was parked, where it was forbidden, and the woman was pregnant, an officer would understand, that she couldn't walk very far and not give her a ticket.

I loved that people could keep their human side and wouldn't be expected to function like machines.

Shift

I thought there was one thing though, that Greece hadn't been able to teach me. That was to think in terms of *we* and *us*, instead of *I* and *me*. While Greeks were thinking for the whole family, I kept thinking as an individual and going my own way.

Now, once again, I was ready to continue my own path into an unknown future. Still I was here, enjoying it as much as I could.

Summer in Greece is a pleasant time. When friends come together, they usually end up sitting around a large table full of good food and wine. They eat and drink and when it gets good, they philosophize or sing, as hours go by.

"Could it get any better than this?" I was wondering.

Interestingly, during the period before my departure the contact to my different teachers fell away. Communication seemed suddenly funny or impossible. It was like life was telling me that I had received the teachings and that I had to rely on myself and my own knowing now.

As time passed, the date for my departure came closer. On my way to New Zealand I wanted to stop over in India and Bali and spend 2-3 months traveling before getting back to the backpacker's hostel and work. On my way back to Europe I planned to visit the Fiji Islands and California. Altogether I was going to be away for nearly one year.

I would have liked to make my choices, as I was going along and decide at each moment, where to go next, but the cheaper way to travel was on a round-the-world-ticket, which meant that I had to decide for the route beforehand. Still it would leave me my free choice, where to go once I was in a country.

My partner said to our friends, "When you love someone you sometimes need to let that person go. She is going to do something great. How could *I* stop her?"

37

We agreed to give each other our absolute freedom and see where we would find ourselves after my journey.

I played my part in all this, as if I hadn't seen the truth already, just because the play had to be played chapter by chapter. My partner played his part magnificently.

I suggested we meet on Bali and have a holiday together, but he wasn't sure whether he was going to make it.

I closed my eyes and asked my heart, "Where do I go first?" The answer that came up was, "Himalaya!"

"Wow, right to the top-right into the highest region of our lovely planet", I thought. I loved the idea and got all excited!

So I booked another flight from Delhi to Leh in Ladakh. I chose the same date for my departure, on which I once had left my home country to travel the world; the 15th August. It was like symbolically saying, that I would now continue the trip that I had once started.

I didn't have a big farewell party. Instead, I saw my friends one at a time. The goodbyes were many. My dearest friends gave me a photo for my little album. In it, I carried the pictures of the people I loved most. This way I felt they were with me where ever I would go.

* * *

Note: I was in Greece before the economic and political crisis became such an issue. Things became really difficult for many people after I had left. I sometimes wonder about the timing of my inner call to move somewhere else and about how thoughts create a reality. I often ask myself if the choices I had made and my thoughts around how to live my life didn't resonate anymore with the outer reality that would be created in Greece.

High Altitude

*T*he flight over the Himalayas was stunning. It looked like a never-ending ocean of mountains to me, covering the whole horizon. I felt my solar plexus contracting. How would I get out of there again? Were there any roads down there?

I knew, there were and the drive would take two days. I didn't like the idea and noticed I felt a little scared.

My worries were interrupted by a voice, asking: "Would you like water or lemonade?" Lemonade sounded good but I got a big surprise: it tasted sweet, sour and *salty*! I tried again but I just couldn't get used to that taste!

When the plane landed in Leh, it was still early in the morning. I had heard, some people throw up, when they leave the plane because of the sudden change to the high altitude. Luckily I was alright, especially, as I was coming from a town by the sea, which meant altitude zero.

It is recommended to just chill out for the first week, when you get to Leh and adapt to the high altitude. A friendly taxi-driver took me to the hotel of my choice and after I had settled into my room, I thought of nothing else but relaxing and adapting to the new climate. It went quite well for a while, but besides all my good intentions it was impossible for me to be still. I was too excited to find out what the town had to offer. Soon I was out on the road and walking around the streets, with all its little shops and restaurant. Tourism seemed to be the major source of income here, and parts of the town had developed around it. There were many travel agencies and tour operators.

It is always interesting to see what resonates with us when we are in a new place. The hotel where I was staying was nice and my room was looking out at its large vegetable garden, but to stay there on a longer term exceeded my budget. I kept my eyes open to see if I could find another accommodation. I kept walking around and checked out numerous other guesthouses until I found a really nice one with peaceful surroundings and a room with a lot of space to do my yoga practice. The place basically was a family home that was turned into a guesthouse during the tourist season and the room that I had chosen used to be one of their private rooms. It had no bed but a mattress on the floor what suited me well.

The landlady was keen for me to stay. There was only one problem, she said. At the moment, someone else was staying in the room but I could have it after a few days and we agreed on that.

On the way back to my hotel, I saw all these signs for trekking and finally asked one of the agents for further information. When I said that I had just arrived and wouldn't be able yet to get on any high mountain trek, I was told that there were routes along the valley that I could easily do. I said, I would think about it and went off to have a "chai" somewhere. I suddenly felt very tired and needed a rest.

As I was sipping on my spicy tea, I considered how it would suit me to go trekking while my room was still occupied. Booking a guided tour with a group of people wasn't really what I wanted. I needed to be out there on my own and not be forced to eventually listen to the chatter of others. I liked the idea of staying with local families along the way to see how they were living. It also meant I wouldn't need to carry much luggage with me as food would be provided.

When I finally got back to my room, my head was aching. It reminded me that I was supposed to just sit around quietly on my first day.

The next day, after finishing my morning yoga practice and having some breakfast, I went back to one of the offices, which had a big sign for homestays. I told the agent that I wanted to book a tour on an easy trek along the valley and he suggested to me which villages I could stay in. He gave me some vouchers. On each of them he had written (in letters I could not read) the name of the family, who would be my host. He assured me that it was easy to follow the trek, as it was the only one there and easy to see. I also would meet other people along the way and would have no problem.

"Don't you have any map for me?" I asked.

He finally gave me a brochure with further information that showed that I would head through the Snow Leopard National Park. It also had a drawing of the trek. To my surprise, I saw that there were two mountain passes on my trek.

"No problem" the agent said, "They are not difficult." He marked the villages, where I would stay and booked a taxi for me to get me to the first village early the next morning. Confident and happy to be soon *out there*, I left the office.

In the evening, I climbed the many steps up to one of the Stupas, from where I could watch the sunset. The view over the valleys and mountain ranges was amazing. I found a quiet corner away from the crowds to do some mantra chanting, as the sun was setting.

I was pleased that my body had had no difficulty to get up there, and it was only my second day in high altitude.

*   *   *

The village where the taxi dropped me off the next morning consisted of a few houses. The driver pointed in the direction of where I would find a bridge to pass the river. Not knowing, where exactly I was going, I headed off, a light daypack on my shoulders and—yes—there was a bridge to cross the Indus River.

"The Indus River" I thought. I had heard about the ancient civilisations in the Indus Valley. Now I was there!

No one else was in sight, as I walked along the river, with its roaring sound in my ears. To my disappointment the path left the river soon and went uphill. The land was dry and dusty like a desert, a rocky mountain desert. I could see a dirt road further up. I followed the narrow trek for as long as I could, avoiding the road. I came to a round stone wall, with a small shelter that obviously was there for animals and their shepherd. Soon I was high above the Indus and came to a point, where the path went right along the edge and felt really dangerous. I now had to continue on the road. This path looked, as if it was made for mountain goats only.

I took a risk and went straight up the short slope. The ground was soft and not solid. Should I slide, I would go right over the edge, I realized. My heart started to pump from anxiety but, too late, I was already doing it!

Luckily everything went alright. It made me aware though, that I mustn't take risks like this. I had been tired and not wanting to go back to find a better spot to reach the road. I decided to be more careful in the future.

The sun was burning down and I fixed my long scarf under my cap and around my head to protect me from it. It didn't look very elegant, but here there were other priorities.

After a while, the road entered a narrow valley with a small creek. Here I found a small path that went in and out and along the creek. I took off my shoes to cool my feet in the refreshing water. Yes, that was better! I threw water all over my head and face, and let my hands and arms hang into the cooling wetness. I wondered how many hours I had been hiking for? Only three.

I told myself, "you better continue!" I hadn't met anyone so far, just the mountains and me, as I had wanted it. For a moment I stood and breathed in the wide space, waiting for—I don't know what, actually. Then I went on. After a while, the valley made a turn and suddenly there were trees—many trees! It got even better; trees full of small, round apricots! Yum, they were ripe and sweet. That was an oasis in the mountain desert!

I filled my stomach and lay down on a patch of grass, on the ground. I must have fallen asleep. When I woke up there was a local woman not far from me, picking all the apricots that had fallen onto the ground. I went over and helped her. She didn't speak to me, but she naturally accepted my help. When we had filled all her baskets, she simply nodded her head towards me and left.

A few hours later, I arrived at the first village. Most people were in the fields, bringing in the harvest of the year. Summers are very short in Ladakh. So is the farming season and a lot of work needs to be done then. I met an elderly man and showed him the name of the family, written on my voucher. He showed me their house.

The daughter of the family welcomed me. Luckily she was at home, because she was the only one that spoke a little bit of English. She leaded me into a small room, which had large windows, looking out at the mountains and three mattresses on the floor. I was left to rest and soon she came back, with a huge thermos filled with sweet tea and some biscuits.

Gratefully, I stretched out, enjoying the simple comfort and the hot tea. That felt so good! Suddenly, I saw a flea jumping at me. I decided to not to make it a big deal, as there was nothing I could do about it.

Later, I sat in the large kitchen and living room. On one side of the room all the cupboards were filled with copper and brass pots. The grandfather of the family simply sat on the floor in the middle of the room. He didn't speak or do anything. I was shown, where to sit and watched the young woman making a dough, which she formed into small balls. Later, they would be cooked in a soup for dinner.

As it got dark, the rest of the family came home from their work in the fields and we had our meal: soup and chapati. After dinner the daughter and I sat together teaching each other English and Ladakhi language.

The next morning, I got up early, with a long hike in front of me. I was a little bit worried about the pass. It said 4950m on the map and it was only my fourth day in high altitude.

Chapatis were made for breakfast and I was told to take some with me for lunch.

When I left the village, the path led into a wide, mainly dry riverbed and I got lost somewhere there. I kept following the riverbed. After a while, I saw a farmer working in his small field. I pointed ahead asking for the village I had to reach next. The man shook his head and pointed backwards and up the hill.

"Oh no" I thought. "How far did I have to go back?" "For how long had I been heading in the wrong direction?"

Luckily it wasn't too bad. Soon I saw the trek winding itself up the mountain. The trek soon became a narrow fine line along the wide slope. Breathing became harder and I had to slow down.

After another hour, I felt totally exhausted and had to rest. The sun was burning down and I squeezed myself into the narrow shade of a big rock. Suddenly, I could hear voices and laughter and saw a group of hikers coming down the hill. They were all fully equipped with sticks and the right gear (probably all members of an alpine club). Obviously they were having a lot of fun, as they went down fast. With sympathy they looked at me, as I continued my struggle uphill.

A mantra formed in my head, "Keep going, keep breathing." "Keep going, keep breathing." Step by step, I fought myself up the mountain. From time to time, I stood just to catch my breath. I then heard someone whistle and saw a local man with his ponies coming up the trek. As he passed me, he saw that I was struggling and offered to take my backpack for me. He spoke a little bit of English and told me he was a guide on his way to meet a French mountain climber.

Gratefully, I gave him my bag that by now felt a hundred kilos heavy. He swung it onto his back and I followed him, trying to stay behind him. As there was no chance for me to keep up with him, I saw my bag being carried away from me. He must have seen the worry in my face and stopped to wait for me. He rolled a cigarette while I came slowly closer. On the next platform, I pulled out my camera to take a photo of the stunning mountain site. He asked if I was ok and when I said "yes", we went on. Soon he was far ahead of me again like a mountain goat, home in this altitude. I started to feel really dizzy and I was suddenly not ok. It is a weird sensation, when you breathe and breathe and don't get the oxygen you need! I was trying not to panic.

The local man was already further up the hill and when I thought that he was looking in my direction, I waved my arms at him, trying to signal: help!

Thank God he came and he held my arm to help me. Under normal conditions, I wouldn't allow any local man to touch me, but this was different. He noticed how cold my skin felt and started rubbing my hands. I stood and breathed and breathed and breathed. When he asked me if I could go on, I pointed at a rock, 5 steps away and said, "OK, until there!"

I made it and needed to stop again in order to catch my breath. We went on like this in 10 step intervals and finally made it to the pass. A cold wind nearly blew me over. There was a shelter though and we sat down in the shade of the wind. I was too exhausted to eat anything, but he convinced me to have some food. So I ate a little. When I opened my bag, I saw a book and my journal and asked myself, why I was carrying this extra weight with me.

After a while, we carried on. Downhill it went a little better. I felt still quite weak, but the pony guide had already given me a lot of his time and he needed to get on faster. He was already late and the French hiker was probably waiting for him. So I let him go, not without thanking him, but how do you thank someone who perhaps saved your life?

Words say so little but the thank you will always be in the heart!

Alone, I had to keep the panic under control. The physical struggle lay behind me but a feeling of insecurity had stayed with me. It was like little devils had woken up in my mind, and were having a lot of fun by scaring me. I sat down, focusing in order not to 'lose it'.

Then I heard a beloved voice saying to me, "You will be alright." "You'll be alright!"

Breathing in this wonderful message, I felt a relief and trusting it, I got up and back on my way to the next village. I could already see the luscious green fields down in the distant valley.

When I reached the village, I saw a sign saying; homestay. No one was there, when I arrived. I called out and walked around the house. No answer. I looked inside a shed and found several goatskins. I took one, spread it on the ground and sank onto it.

Drifting into a pleasant heaviness, I got a surprise, when I suddenly saw a woman standing in front of me, looking at me full of surprise. At first I couldn't remember where I was.

"Homestay" was all I could say, when I did manage to say something.

"Ah!" a smile appeared in her face. Laughing, she took the goatskin and showed me my room. The toilet was, as usual, a hole in the ground and when I asked where to wash, she pointed at the creek near by.

On my travels in India I had seen local women, with their bare breasts, washing themselves and their clothes in a river. So I did the same and was not bothered if anyone saw me. It felt good to wash the dust out of my hair too, even if I had nothing else but cold water.

When I got back to my room, the thermos with hot tea was already there. Gratefully, I felt the hot liquid entering my body and enjoyed everything about it, while I looked out through the large windows at the bizarre mountain site. The bedrooms here seemed all to have the same style, with large windows, a low table and mattresses on the floor. I sank on one of them and soon felt bitten by something. Once again, I saw a flea jumping at me. Would that be the same everywhere?

As I was resting, I still could feel that sense of insecurity, and I didn't feel well at all. To distract my mind, I took out my book and when I opened it, I was amazed to read the heading of the next chapter. It said, "The human fear"!!

Reading it, I understood why I needed to have this book with me. It taught me how fear and love are the opposite powers of the universe. There could only be one feeling at the time in us: either love or fear. To control any fear, I needed to connect deeply with my heart and fill it with love. So there was no space left for fear.

How could I awaken the feeling of love and fill my heart with love right now? I thought of my daughter and felt my heart filling with love. I thought of my partner, my family and my dearest friends and felt it further filling with love. I thought of Jason in New Zealand, the man I had felt so passionate about. Passion has an immense power, and I tried to use it here to my advantage. To nourish my heart even more, I started writing down my dream life with him, and because there was no reality to it, I could go fully into the fantasy of it. I dived into the dream and bathed myself in the beautiful feelings, generated by it. The very best love life I could imagine became the next chapter in my own journal. How good I had my journal with me!

I went into every little detail of our happy life together, enjoying the nice feeling created by it. Bathing myself in the feeling of love, I washed the fear and insecurity away. I realized what the insecurity had originally been: Fear—fear of dying! Oops, just thinking that brought the fear immediately back. "No fear—only love" became my mantra for the night.

*   *   *

The next day turned out to be just joyful. It was my turn to enjoy the hike downhill. The trek went along a gorge, with amazing rock formations, and all kind of shapes. This time, *I* felt like a mountain goat, moving and jumping along with ease.

In my fingertips, bum and under my skin, I had a funny tingling, electric sensation. The blood flow was obviously increasing in the limbs of my body, pouring into all the fine blood vessels again. Life was coming back to me.

By lunchtime, I had reached the next village, where two treks were crossing each other. Beside homestays it had a few 'restaurants', which in the Himalayas often consist of a parachute tent. I found a small shop in a tiny stone house that also had a 'restaurant' sign, and was happy to have a cooked meal, instead of chapatis with rank butter.

Two more hikers and their guide came along, and now I didn't mind to have a chat. One of them said, "Oh, you're hiking all by yourself! We were just talking about how crazy and dangerous that is!"

"You might be right but I really wanted to be alone out here—just me and the vast space, you see" I replied. And when I told them about my little adventure the day before, and how at the right time this pony guide had come along, they said, "Well, you were lucky. Good, you're here now and it turned out fine, but your heart could just have stopped, you know?"

How good I didn't know. I probably would have panicked much more!

*　　*　　*

The fleas were bad that night in my room. They were many and kept me agitated. Sleep didn't come easily. My mind felt agitated too. I had to get over another mountain pass tomorrow. This time it would be rather a psychological challenge than a physical. The pass wasn't that high, but the memory of the last pass brought the fear and insecurity right back to me.

"Only love—no fear!" I kept to my mantra the next day. I needed to fully concentrate on the feeling of love, as I once again was out there all by myself.

"Only love—no fear!" I went on and after a while the words of a song formed in my head, "Love is like oxygen".

"Yes, love is like oxygen", I said to myself and oxygen was what I needed. Repeating the two mantras, I climbed up the mountain. Suddenly the melody and a phrase of another song popped into my mind ". . . . it's easy to do! . . . ." Hanging on to this mantra, I reached the pass *easily*. It really worked; I had no breathing difficulties and made it with ease to the top. With a sense of victory, I took a photo of myself on top of the pass. When I looked at it later I—for the first time—saw the writing on my cap. The letters had been embroidered in exactly the same colour on the cap and weren't very visible. What did it say? *No Fear!*

From the pass it wasn't very far downhill until I reached the Zanskar River. I had been told that I would have to pay to pass the bridge. Now I saw what "the bridge" actually was: a wooden box, hanging on an iron rope. It was pulled by two men over the river—one on each side.

I had to wait until it reached my side. A load of large sacks with all kinds of contents came with it. After it was emptied, it was my turn to jump inside. I asked for a photo shot. Then, I was pulled over the river. Looking at the strong currents below me, and the rope above me, I thought, "That won't break, will it?"

I trusted that it wouldn't and relaxed. The sacks had been much heavier than me. Still it felt exciting and taking the excitement with me, I jumped off at the other side.

Arriving at the other side was like arriving back in civilisation. An asphalt road brought jeeps and rafting groups into the region, and all of a sudden, I was surrounded by a real buzz.

It was a short walk along the road to the next village and my last homestay. From there I would take the bus back into town the very next day. It was only midday, when I arrived and I had plenty of time to myself. I watched the farmers separating the wheat from the chaff, by throwing it into the air with a dung fork just like farmers in Europe had done hundred years ago. Here, away from the road, the place was quiet again.

A huge tree with soft grass under it looked so inviting, that I lay down in its shade, resting my body and soul. Listening to the running water of the near by creek, and listening to the wind in the trees, was like listening to the sound of eternity.

And as I was lying there just listening, I got carried back in time to my childhood. I saw myself doing the same thing; lying by a river under a tree, listening to the sound of wind and water and the silent sound beyond: eternity.

Once again, I felt like the child carried and embraced by the earth under me, touched and caressed by the soft wind. I felt open, loved, connected to mother, father, all that is.

I felt peace—deep peace.

*   *   *

The bus the next day was late. When it finally came only a couple from France and I got on the bus. All the locals who had been waiting with us were just picking up food supply.

The bus driver played around with a tape recorder and some cassettes until he had found, what he had been looking for. Songs, sung by a woman in a very high voice, accompanied our ride through a rocky valley back into town. I was enjoying it: music!

Along the road I saw signs in English, saying things like, "If you're married divorce speed", "Hurry brings worry" and "Driving and Whisky is risky".

In spite of it we soon reached the scene of an accident. Another bus stood deserted in the middle of the road, and a jeep was lying upside down in the gorge below.

51

We saw a local woman standing on the side of the road, and looking down at it. She seemed horrified.

We all were horrified. Was that the bus that was supposed to pick us up this morning? Was that the reason, why we had to wait for so long?

On my previous trips to India and Nepal I had seen other bus accidents and I had heard of many more. The point was to be always on "the right" bus.

We however reached Leh safely. I went back to the agent that had booked my homestays on the trek, in order to tell him off for sending me over a high mountain pass when I had asked for an 'easy trek' along the valley.

He was half smiling, when he said, "At least you had an unforgettable adventure!"

Yes, that was definitely the case. He had a point there that I couldn't deny. Then he asked, "How did you get over the river?"

"I used *the bridge*, as you had told me", I answered.

"Oooh, you were lucky because the bridge broke and other people had difficulties to pass the river. They had to hire a boat and pay a lot of money!"

Thinking of the moment, when I sat in this wooden box wondering, if the iron rope might break or not, I couldn't be less concerned about money. Thanks God, 'the bridge' had worked for me!

Grateful, that I had come back from my adventure alive and unharmed, I went back to the guesthouse to find, that my room was still occupied. The landlady promised that it would soon be empty, and suggested I relax and have some chai first.

While I got comfortable on the soft cushions and had my tea, I heard the hustle and rustle of things being moved, and hoped that I didn't cause any trouble to one of the other guests.

Soon the room was ready for me to move in, and I at last could make myself at home. I asked for permission to hang up some small signs for massage therapy that I carried with me. Hopefully, I would have some work, while I stayed here. The landlady was offering breakfast and simple meals in their living room, and it felt a little weird to see that the whole family slept on the kitchen floor during this period. Still they all seemed happy and eager to please us, the guests.

During breakfast the next morning, I got to meet the other guests. We soon became friends and started to go out and do things together.

It was the time of the annual Cultural Festival of Ladakh. Together we went to the opening parade of the festival, to music and dance performances. Together we watched and finally had our go in the archery competition. Once again, I enjoyed how open people who travel are and how easily communication flows. It's like we all belong to the same family. Some of them booked in for a massage with me, which was great. They either paid me with money or a shared dinner.

There was only one thing that I didn't share with them, and that was the joint or the pipe that often was going around. My joint was yoga and I chose to get "high" by uplifting my energy level to a higher frequency through the practice of asana, pranayama and mantra chanting. The serenity of the high mountains was the ideal environment for that.

*   *   *

Borderline

My days could have carried on in their peaceful way, but I decided to do another tour to the Pangong Lake. I had heard a lot about the breath taking beauty of the large saltwater lake that runs right into Tibet. To visit the lake would require a permit from the police station. I would also need to find some more people to share a jeep.

The easiest way was to go through a local agent and I decided to give it another try but chose a different one this time. Within two days he had got a small group together and had done all the necessary arrangements. It was early in the morning and still dark when the jeep left Leh with five of us.

The road went over the world's third highest pass Chang La. A slight dizziness came along with the altitude but it was bearable. A military camp was set up on the pass. Our driver had to report who we were, where we were going and show our permits. We used the opportunity to visit the toilet, which was the by far the ugliest I had seen in my life. Luckily, the boys could just use the big one outside.

Heading down on the other side of the pass, we came around a corner and had a first glance of the stunning looking lake. We stopped where a shallow stream crossed the road, and had a walk around to refresh ourselves.

When we finally reached the lake, it was early afternoon. The village that was our destination had two buildings and a couple of tents. It was the first village right by the lake. We had a look around and weren't impressed. A 'Restaurant' offered tea, coffee, breakfast, lunch, dinner and an overnight stay.

There was another village seven kilometres further along the shore, and that was as far as we were allowed to go. Beyond there was China.

We told our driver that we would walk there. Full of excitement and happy to move we left. The air was chilly. I thought I could smell snow.

The road led through several riverbeds, and we tried hard to jump from rock to rock and keep our feet dry. One of the guys was often slow to understand what was going on and made us laugh a lot. It all happened in a sweet and friendly way. Luckily, he didn't mind.

By the time we arrived at the next village, we were all exhausted. Walking in high altitude was still tiring. The place looked deserted. It took us a while to find some local people and ask them for accommodation. We finally followed a sign saying 'Guesthouse', which led us to a family home, with a few rooms on the first floor. They looked inviting enough for us to stay, and we didn't have much choice anyway.

Soon, some hot tea arrived and, as we were sipping it, we became all happy again. The altitude made us feel lightheaded. One of the guys, who was Indian, had a good sense of humour. He made us crack-up laughing constantly.

Thinking about my last mountain trip, where I had avoided company, I realized that that was something I couldn't do, when I was alone: make myself laugh in such a way! It finally wasn't necessarily bad to have the chatter of others in my company!

It came to my mind that somewhere I had read, "In our laughter is God's breath!" If this is right, I was definitely in divine company!

* * *

The next morning, the sun was out and I made us jump into the icy cold water of the lake.

At first, the others didn't seem to like the idea. Especially the Indian guy was used to bathe in much warmer water, but he was also of very enthusiastic nature and when he saw me splashing around, he just had to follow. In the end, we were all splashing around, laughing and screaming because of the cold. We didn't last long, but had still our fun, and probably disturbed the peace of the lake with our noisiness.

On our drive back to Leh, we saw that all the mountaintops had snow. Summer was over. It was time to leave before the roads out of Ladakh would officially close.

Back in Leh, we met a friend, who was just leaving for Srinagar. "Where is Srinagar?" I asked. "Oh Srinagar is in Kashmir. It's supposed to be one of the most beautiful places on earth."

One of the most beautiful places on earth . . . That sounded like me. Should I go there too?

I had always assumed I would leave Ladakh on the road to Manali that led southward. I had never thought of going west to Kashmir. The situation in Kashmir was politically unstable. The conflict between India and Pakistan around Kashmir was not resolved. Still other travellers went there. Things had quietened down, I was told. At the moment, the countries were negotiating with each other and it was relatively safe for traveling.

Two days later, I found myself on a bus to Srinagar. Next to me sat a guy from France. We tried to have a conversation, me with the little French I could remember and he with his broken English, but soon we fell silent following our own thoughts.

I had the window seat and thus the view to an incredible beautiful mountain site and into the valley of the Indus River. After a while, the lower set of the mountains changed its colour into a sandy yellow that reminded me of a moonscape. The land was sculptured by wind and rain into the most bizarre forms and shapes. Soon we reached the bus stop of the small town Lamayuru. To my great joy and surprise, one of the friends I had made in Leh entered the bus. Already twice before we had said goodbye, and then bumped into each other again.

From there, the road went through a narrow gorge and became quite narrow itself. At times I couldn't see it anymore, as it seemed to disappear somewhere under the bus, me looking straight into the gorge. The image of the jeep that had gone over the edge, after crashing into the bus, and similar other stories came into my mind. I watched the bus driver constantly turning his head to the fellow next to him, as they were chatting away.

Then, we met a truck and couldn't get passed it. Both drivers tried to maneuver their vehicles around to get passed each other. I sat at the end of the bus, right above the wheel, and opened my window to have a better look. We were going backwards, and the wheel was only a meter away from the edge.

"Stop!", I screamed as loud as I could, and the bus stopped with its back wheel about thirty centimetres away from the edge. I finally lost my temper, and asked to get off the bus, while they were manoeuvring. At that moment, the bus driver drove a little forward, and at last the truck driver managed to get by.

I could hardly relax after this incident. Especially, as I saw another truck lying deep down at the bottom of the gorge. I wished, I had a seat on the other side of the bus, looking at the mountain or that I could just sleep like many of the Indian passengers did.

Once again, I saw myself having to deal with the fear of dying. I believed in the eternity of my soul and in reincarnation. My body though, didn't want to die. I felt its strong instinct for survival, and the adrenalin level rising in my blood, and making my heart pump wildly.

I closed my eyes and tried once again to focus on the feeling of love. This time, I found it much harder, to feel the relief and the joy of love filling me. My mind kept telling me, that it wasn't up to me, but up to the bus driver, whether I'd reach Srinagar safely or not. There was absolutely nothing I could do about it. Or could I? What if I mentally send some good energy to the bus driver? I had the second degree of Reiki, a healing method that uses universal energy for healing, and had learned how to use it for treatments from a distance. So I sent Reiki to the driver and my prayers to heaven.

Luckily, the road soon became wider and less high and I started to feel safer.

Out of Kargil, we all had to get off the bus into the cold of the late afternoon for a military check. Kargil is the most northern town in India close to the border with Pakistan.

One of the foreigners had obviously offended the officials by not answering one of the questions on the form. We soon got to understand, that this was serious business! The officer in charge shouted at him and got so mad, that he didn't seem able to stop himself again. I stood two meters away from the scene and felt pushed to try calming him down. Discretely, I stepped closer and used a Buddhist practice, I had once learned, called "Tonglen". I started breathing in the energy of hot, heavy, dark and breathed out bright, light and cooling energy towards the officer.

A moment later, the officer suddenly turned around and looked at me. I will never forget this look. It was brief and full of surprise. He then let go of the guy.

We stopped for the night in Drass, where a former boarding school next to our bus stop served as 'hotel'. I paired up with another woman from Germany, to share a room and save money. The room had no electricity or water. We both had a candle and thus no problem to bring some light into the place. That there was no water bothered us more, as it made the use of the attached toilet very unpleasant. We both had been in India for a while and knew it was better to take it with humour.

When we went for dinner that night, together with my French seat neighbour and the friend from Leh who was Canadian, we laughed a lot. From then on, the four of us formed a new group and did everything together. The way every adventure had a new combination of people sharing it, reminded me of playing dice: with every throw you get a new combination of numbers. Likewise we travellers were thrown together in different combinations, to share a certain experience of our journey.

This journey started again at 3 o'clock am. Due to strict military regulations the bus had to clear the pass on our way by 5 am.

Soon I realized, that I had left my only shawl behind. The shawl had been a gift from a friend in Greece and had protected me from sun and wind on my trek through the mountains. I noticed with surprise how I nearly felt angry, that I had forgotten it. Wow—I had created an attachment here (!) and attachment leads to suffering, as I knew.

"Let go—let go!" I told myself. "Things come and go. Let them come and go!"

* * *

59

When we finally reached Srinagar, Kashmir's summer capital, the town was full of military people. Walls of sand sacks were lining the road. They could be used as barricades at any time, and also served for the protection from flying bullets in case of shootings.

I felt anyway grateful, that I had survived the bus trip. Like most of the travellers, the four of us wanted to stay on a houseboat. There are stories of travellers being captured on houseboats by food poisoning, by confiscation of their passports or lies about violence onshore. Luckily, my Canadian friend had an address from a friend of a houseboat at the far end of the Dal Lake in a quiet and peaceful setting. The four of us decided to check it out, and finally rented it together.

The houseboat turned out to be like a floating villa, with two large bedrooms and a lounge, all with beautiful woodcarvings. When we sat down for tea on the little veranda overlooking the lake, I thought that I was dreaming. It was so beautiful.

Soon we were approached by a gondola, here called "shikara" and offered a ride for a good price to one of the Mughal gardens on the other side of the lake. Enthusiastically, we jumped into the boat. Two of us had to sit, while the other two could stretch out on a large upholstered seat.

I got to lie down first and again thought I was dreaming. Feeling like a queen, I fully relaxed into the beauty of the mirror-like water, parts of it covered in lotus flowers. We had just missed the blossoming season of the lotus, but there were still some remains of it.

The Kashmiri man stopped rowing and picked some. He made a bouquet and gave it to me. Then he showed us the floating gardens and explained how they work. It was amazing to see anything grow there on the little bit of floating soil like in a real garden.

As we got closer to the other side of the lake, we passed other "shikaras" with local people staring at us.

A little later, I started to feel unwell. First I noticed a change in my energy. The blissful feeling was gone. Instead I felt my whole body slightly aching.

In the Mughal Garden, I ran straight to the toilet and just made it before the diarrhoea overcame me. From there I dragged myself around, feeling dizzy and weak.

On our shikara ride back to the houseboat, I was shivering. When we got there I again had to occupy the bathroom. Luckily the sink was right in front of the toilet because I was throwing up and shitting all at the same time. It was awful.

What had happened to me? I had eaten exactly the same food as my friends. Had I caught "the evil eye"?

I crept into bed and slept deliriously until the next morning.

When I woke up I felt better, but still sick. At least, I thought, I was in the perfect place for being sick: in a clean, beautiful and spacious environment, with friends around me. That was comforting.

I didn't mind staying in bed and getting better. In the afternoon, I even got up and sat with the others on the balcony by the water. Another boat approached and we heard a voice saying, "I am the delicious man!"

"Delicious man?" we laughed. He smiled and slowly opened the box in front of him and showed us chocolate, biscuits and small cakes.

My friends became very happy. I retreated back to bed—too early for me to have these kinds of treats!

Until I was well enough to go to town things were coming to me. Different dealers came along on their boats trying to sell souvenirs and saffron. The delicious man came every day. He knew what he was doing. Most of the foreigners staying at the other end of the lake, were smoking pot and craving sweets. In fact that was what once again created a separation between my friends on the houseboat and me. I wasn't interested and so we were functioning from a different level of awareness, like we lived in different worlds.

We had our own cook Mohammad, a Muslim like most Kashmiris, on board. He was preparing lovely meals for us. Some of them I could eat. Thus, there was no need for any food shopping.

When I was feeling better, Mohammad said we should go into town, because the following day we wouldn't be able to. One of the Indian ministers was coming to Srinagar and it would be difficult to get around due to police controls. Some streets would be closed for safety reasons. When we asked him about his opinion of the political situation and whether he would rather be Indian or Pakistani, he said, "We people in Kashmir want to have our own country. We want to be independent!"

We took a rickshaw into town. When I finally left the boat, I became aware that there was a leprosy hospital in our neighbourhood.

Was that the reason why it was so quiet and peaceful at this side of the lake? Were the locals avoiding the area and staying away? Was that the reason why we had been able to rent such a luxury houseboat for so little money?

In town, we were walking around a little bit lost. It had rained and the streets were wet and dirty. Soon we got bored with the market area. Only the French guy was interested in buying a few souvenirs. He would go home soon. The other two and I were traveling around, which meant every piece would become an extra weight in our luggage. I kept my eyes open for a pashmina shawl, but couldn't find one. It would have been the place to buy a carpet, but it wouldn't fit into a suitcase and I was not willing to carry it around with me. We decided to visit another famous Mughal garden.

This one was definitely worth a visit. The creator of this garden must have liked to play with water. Beautiful fountain arrangements were lined up to the walkway. There was a pavilion surrounded by water and an artificial waterfall had attracted a group of young women who were walking slowly along the bluish water in their colourful clothes. The picture looked like a piece of artwork and would have inspired every painter.

It was us though, who attracted all the looks, as there are not many tourists in Kashmir. Soon we found ourselves surrounded by groups of school kids and young adults, who all wanted to have their photo taken with us. They were pushing each other to stand next to us in their enthusiasm. It was funny.

Time passed quickly and in the end we needed to hurry to get back to the lake and catch a shikara back to our boat, as everything shuts down early in Srinagar.

The next day, I was feeling quite sick again. We had been in one of those very sugary Indian sweetshops on our tour through the market area in town. Or should I say Kashmiri sweetshop? To me there was no difference, as it was all mainly based on sugar and milk.

In general, I started to feel sick of Indian and Kashmiri heavily spiced and oily food. When we were floating along the shore of the lake in a small rowing boat one day, I saw a house that reminded me of a country house in France.

My family has a house in France and since I was a teenager I had been visiting France. The picture of French cheese, baguette and red wine popped into my mind. It was the French guy who was rowing the boat and together we indulged in the fantasy of it.

I didn't have them often but there are these moments when a traveller dreams of the food he eats at home, the food he has grown up with. Indian people know this and make a lot of business from it. In tourist places, the restaurants offer a variety of food, from pasta and pizza to falafel and hamburgers. Nearly every dairy sells the chocolate spread Nutella.

But this was Kashmir, and our cook on the houseboat cooked traditionally, which I would have much preferred if I wasn't sick.

It seemed like the time had come to move on. Our Canadian friend had already flown back to Delhi. The rest of us were going to take the bus to Jammu, Kashmir's other capital in the South.

We decided to leave early in the morning and visit the floating market on our way to the bus station. It takes place at six o'clock and doesn't last long. So one needs to be there on time, in order to catch a sight of the full splendour of the colourful event. Instead of stalls, everything is sold from boats and moves around.

It was a magical moment when we crossed the lake just before sunrise. A crescent moon was shining above the mountains. At first, there was deep silence. The oar dipping into the water was the only thing we could hear. Then, all of a sudden, the sound of prayers coming from many different mosques filled the air of the early morning. The skyline over the mountains turned orange and the morning star shone brightly above it.

*   *   *

The road to Jammu was full of military people. An endless number of trucks and buses filled with soldiers were heading north, reminding me that I was in a war zone. It didn't look like the negotiations around Kashmir had led to any improvement or that the conflict had resolved itself. On the contrary, I got the impression more tension was building up. I was glad to be on my way out of there. We had to pass another checkpoint, but as we were leaving, the country the officials were more relaxed this time.

A traveller from the US had filled the gap that our Canadian friend had left in our little group. He joined us during our stop for lunch and stayed with us for the rest of the journey until Jammu where our roads were finally parting. One gets used to constantly saying goodbye to people along the road, and then hello to new ones.

A very gentle and kind Indian man asked me if I also was going to McLeod Ganj, where the residence of His Holiness the Dalai Lama and many other Tibetan refugees is.

After the Himalayas in Ladakh, that had been my next heart call. My spontaneous visit to Kashmir had been a surprise to me.

Yes, that was where I was going, I answered to the man.

The ride on the night bus to Dharamsala in Himachal Pradesh was bumpy. I was thrown around on my bed and hardly got any sleep. The bus didn't actually go to Dharamsala, but stopped in some place not far from it at 3 o'clock in the morning. Two taxi-jeeps were already waiting in the sleepy, deserted place to pick up any night arrivals. One of them took two foreign couples. The Indian man, me and four guys from Israel were left for the other jeep but the driver wanted to take only me and the Israelis. I was trying to negotiate with him, to take the kind Indian too, but he wouldn't. It hurt me in my soul to watch the Indian man left behind alone in the empty streets, looking at us with big eyes of sorrow as we drove away.

*   *   *

65

Monks and Monkeys

*T*he Tibetan Buddhist Monastery between McLeod Ganj and Bhagsu had a guesthouse. One of the signs said, "Be clean and peaceful please".

A smiling monk welcomed me and showed me my room on the first floor, where all the foreigners were staying. It was simple, had two single beds in it, needed some cleaning as most of the cheaper rooms in India do and the walls showed signs of dampness, but altogether it seemed alright.

I signed in and the smiling monk gave me my keys. "Be careful, don't go along the road alone when it's dark!" he said. "Some women had problem!"

"Ok!" I simply promised.

In the mornings before sunrise, I sat with the monks in the temple while they were doing their chanting. I couldn't follow their chanting so I simply chanted OM. The vibrations created were so powerful, that I could feel different things happening in my body. Releases of tension took place in muscles and other tissues. It was wonderful. Their healing effect was amazing. Within days the last symptoms of the sickness that had still lingered around, finally disappeared.

One morning, I saw a spider the size of my hand sitting at the window of my door as I left my room. I had left the window open through the night. I have an issue with spiders, I must say. Now, I was horrified especially as this one was huge. During the chanting I imagined the spider crawling out of the window and out of my room. When I went back it really was gone! Needless to say, I never left the window open again.

In the afternoons the clouds built up against the hillside, until they finally burst into heavy rain. At some stage before or after the rain, a large group of monkeys would pass through. One day, I had left the door open while having a relaxation on my bed. I heard a banging noise and when I opened my eyes a big monkey was standing in the middle of my room, just stealing my fruit.

"Enjoy your meal", I thought. I wouldn't mess with him!

I also realised I needed to relax about the spiders. There was another big one sitting in the corner of the toilet door. It sat always in the same place and gave me a chance to look at it while doing my business. A couple of weeks went by like this until it finally ran along the wall when I was trapped in position, scaring me to death. That was the end of my spider therapy. I called the smiling monk to get it. He came along with a stick and with the stick he "guided" it out of the toilet and over the veranda into the bush. No killing, no hassle—it left with so much ease!

"Ooh—spider is so small and you're so big!" he laughed. He was so right! Why wasn't I aware of that?

* * *

Without any special reason, I felt very light and happy in McLeod Ganj. I was thinking of all the prayers and chanting the monks in this place do for the liberation of suffering of all people, of all "sentient beings" as they call it. Was that the reason why I felt so good?

Was it possible to *feel* the effect of prayers?

67

When I went to the teachings the abbot or "Rinpoche" of the monastery was giving on the basic ideas of Buddhism, there was a small incident that seemed to confirm this.

I was lying on my bed one day before the class. Suddenly, I felt the presence of an energy with me there and beautifully bathed in it. I thought of the Rinpoche preparing for the teaching and just knew that this energy was coming from him. Was he preparing us students too by sending *something* out to us?

I wished that one day soon, all the prayers for the freedom of suffering, will work for the Tibetan people and monks themselves, who are still occupied, suppressed and tortured by the Chinese government. While I was there, one monk, who was imprisoned and tortured by the Chinese in Tibet/China for sixteen years before he escaped, was just selling his book telling his tremendous story.

The picture of Tibetan monks walking in the streets is somehow part of the town. So are the beggars, some of them the victims of leprosy, reaching out, especially to us foreigners.

I will never forget the old woman stretching her rotten, sometimes badly bandaged, arms into my face whenever I walked by. Some days she was lucky to be the one I would give to. I had a rule to give everyday some money to one person, whoever moved my heart on that day. This way I kept my heart open to help, without getting desperate about the many poor people I couldn't help.

One day, I was pulled into a shop by a woman with a small baby in her arms to buy her some food. I bought her a bag of rice and some milk powder that she wanted, just to find myself approached by the next mother after leaving the shop. In fact there were many of them. They all belonged to the same tribe, living a little outside of town, as I saw later.

I said, "No, I'm sorry!" to the young mother but she wouldn't let go of me. I repeated what I had already said, a little firmer. She insisted pulling at my arm, so I had to use the little "street-Hindi" I had learned and told her to give it up now. After telling her several times in Hindi not to touch me and to give it up, I finally became loud and started yelling at her in—what came spontaneously out of my mouth—as Greek. That helped! She anxiously looked around and finally let go of me.

It hurts to be that strict, but I had once been given that advice by a Swami and yoga teacher, and it always worked.

"At first be polite" he had said "then become strict and if that doesn't help come with the stick!" He 'd been waving his stick around to show that we mustn't be afraid of making some fuss if beggars don't leave us alone.

Not all the beggars were Indian people. Here and there you got a 'Westerner'—as we were usually called—asking for food or help.

Once I sat in a restaurant at the same table with a guy from France, who was telling me he hadn't eaten for days.

"Oh, what would you like to eat?" I asked him and called the waiter to let him order a meal. We sat together for some time talking and when I left, he left too and offered to show me the temple in the complex by the Dalai Lama's residence. I was happy for him to do so.

We passed the building where the monks were active in their practice of debating. They were clapping their hands and stamping their feet while debating with each other, thus reflecting the different voices that often argue inside us. We watched for a while. I wished that I were able to understand, what they were saying.

The temple was sacred to Avalokitesvara, the deity of compassion. Its gilded Buddha statue was huge. I felt emanated by its power, when I sat down in meditation.

After this, what could I say when the French guy asked me if I had a room where he could stay for the night? And it was true there was a second free bed in my room. So I let him stay, but when he asked to stay in the same bed with me I had no problem to say no. I still felt uncomfortable to have him there. I thought, "Okay for one night I can bare it." The next day he didn't seem to want to leave though. Once again I had to be strict.

* * *

In general there was a nice crowd of foreigners in McLeod Ganj. Some cafes had regular open stage nights where people mainly performed music.

Listening to all the people from all over the world made me realize, that we really were a kind of family. In Greece, it had looked a little exotic what I was doing. Here it was just normal. I was amongst people who also were traveling on a discovery of foreign places and themselves. Some guys were Nepali or Indians from the big cities. I became friends with a filmmaker from Delhi. He was a good musician too and well travelled. His points of view were modern and he was very open with people. We sometimes had breakfast together, on the large terrace in the restaurant of his hotel that had an amazing view. He made me listen to some beautiful Indian music on his laptop, very different from what I usually got to hear. I liked his fine sense for beauty and we had a lot of travel experiences to share.

In his company, I went to the local discotheque one night after dinner. It started all well. We were completely enjoying ourselves dancing and as there were a few other female travellers apart from me, we all felt at ease. Some of the Tibetan girls who had been shyly sitting around felt encouraged to get up and dance too. Everybody was having a good time when some Indian tourists started to bother them. Their Tibetan friends came to help and protect them, and before we understood what was going on, we were in the middle of a wild fight between the Indians and the Tibetans. Tables and chairs were flying around. Me and the other foreign girls quickly squeezed ourselves in one corner of the room, trying to stay out of this. Then the owner of the place freaked out. Completely horrified we saw him pulling out a huge sword and hitting it amongst them. Me and the other girls were screaming. He finally hit it hardly on one of the tables and we realized that the blade wasn't sharp. He managed to stop the fight though. Horrified we left. My friend walked me back to the monastery where everything was quiet and peaceful. What a contrast!

I love the contrasts in life. To me there are times for meditation and times for party. I love to embrace the different facets of life. I find a bit of everything is fine. When life offers me a gift, I say thank you, and take it.

The next time, when I saw my friend, I went back with him to his apartment and we had a succulent, sensual night together.

My Greek partner used to compare it with a glass of fresh water someone offers us the moment we are thirsty.

"You take it gratefully and enjoy every drop of it" he used to say.

So here I was, enjoying my glass of water, during a night with no regrets and consequences.

* * *

Everyone was excited: the Dalai Lama would give teachings! I had felt ready to move on but now I would wait. He had just been in Leh before my arrival and I had just missed his teachings. This time I would take the opportunity and see him.

A pass with photo was required beforehand and I queued up together with many others to get it. I was told the teachings would be given in Tibetan language and the translation would be on the radio. So I would need a small transistor.

Many people reserve a seat by placing a piece of cardboard with their name on it in the temple a day before. I just trusted that I would find a good seat by good luck. When I saw the size of the crowd queuing before the temple from the early morning, I wasn't so sure anymore. Our bags and bodies were checked by security stuff before entering the temple. I moved through the mass, whom were already sitting and waiting everywhere around the temple. The inside was reserved for a group from Korea to whom the teachings were given in the first place. I found a place amongst the locals just outside of the main entrance and soon followed their example to sit on the stairs in between all the shoes. From there at least, I had a direct view of the small figure of His Holiness.

I hardly understood a word of his teachings. I pressed my little radio against my ear like most foreigners did but the reception faded constantly. I was told his teachings were very specific on a certain aspect of Buddhism. Never mind, important to me was to be in his presence.

Once, I stood quite close as he was entering. There is something about this shining little man that made my heart open. And this is the gift I took away with me.

I'm not a scholar. Of all the Buddhist teachings, I had read and listened to, in my life, it came down to one thing: loving kindness!

*   *   *

Golden Sunrise

*A*mritsar was my next destination. I had heard the most amazing reports from other travellers about the Golden Temple and to me it has become the holiest place on earth. It took me two buses, one train and a rickshaw to get there. On my arrival, I bought a scarf to cover my head just to find that there were sacks with all kind of head covers at the temple gate for everyone to take for free.

Everyone is welcome at the temple that is the holiest Sikh shrine; no matter what gender, religion or nationality the visitors have. Everyone can stay for three days inside the temple complex and eat whenever hungry. Is there a greater expression of the never-ending source of divine abundance? Where else does a kitchen stay open 24/7, feeding ten thousands of people every day for free? I was deeply impressed.

The chanting inside the beautiful temple began in the early morning and continued until the late evening.

After my long journey and a first visit to the temple, I sank gratefully into my bed in one of the dorms, which were mainly used by foreigners. Most of the Indian pilgrims were sleeping on the ground outside in the open areas.

It was still early when I woke up. I usually start the practice of mantra yoga before getting up. This time, I got up and did the mantras, walking around the pool in which the temple stands. The name of the pool is Amrit Sarovar what means Pool of Nectar.

Aware of each step and repeating the Gayatri and the Mahaamrityunjaya Mantra, I moved around the holy water. It was one of those moments where time stands still. My whole body was permeated by the immense vibration of the place. Step by step, I felt myself getting into a higher state far beyond my physical body, a state of ecstasy that I cannot describe with words. In pure bliss I sat down to watch a golden sunrise above the Golden Temple.

*   *   *

Is there anywhere else to go from here? After encountering the fear of dying in the Himalayan Mountains, after moving through the cycle of sickness in Kashmir and healing in MacLeod Ganj, I had finally come into the holy space of the temple and the holy space of myself where everything shines in a golden light.

I felt, I had found what I was looking for on my journey but as life goes on so does the journey!

Back in the dorms, I met a girl from Israel whom I had already seen in Leh. Together we went to a small park, the Jallianwala Bagh, where the massacre of many Indians by the British army had taken place in 1919. I remembered the horrible scene in the film "Gandhi".

One can still see the bullet marks in a remaining wall that commemorates the event.

After a walk around the park, we lay down on the green grass in the shade to rest. After a while, we heard loud music and went to see what was happening. There was a crowd and a small show going on, which was filmed by probably one of the local TV channels. Young men and woman were dancing. We climbed onto a low wall to have a better view. Now, they were dancing with an orange, a white and a green flag; the colours of the Indian flag. A man did a trick with a portrait of Gandhi and promoted the unity of India. He was pointing out that people from different parts of India were there all together. Then he suddenly pointed at us saying: "Even foreigners are here!"

Suddenly, all the people and the cameras turned on us and we became, to our full surprise, for a moment the centre of everyone's attention.

We looked at each other, wondering if we would be on TV that night.

*   *   *

People were talking about watching the ceremony at the Indian-Pakistan border when the gates get closed for the night.

"You see the Indian people go crazy during the event" someone said. Together with a small crowd I jumped into a taxi, taking us to the only place where one can cross the border between the two countries.

And really, a large crowd had gathered in front of the large gate. The Pakistani side was rather quiet. Was it Ramadan? There were stands, like in a stadium that were filled with people, watching others having their turn to do a run to the gate and back with the Indian flag in their hands. Everyone was cheering, charging the atmosphere with patriotism. Behind the running route a crowd was dancing and jumping around, cheering, shouting and laughing. Then comes the moment of the official ceremony, when the proud commanding officers march up to each other for a handshake and a salute. Bugles blow and the flags are lowered and folded away for the night when the border remains closed.

Amused, I thought how the Indian people turn, even the most serious event, into a party.

*   *   *

Rishikesh

When talking about Rishikesh, the yoga capital, we really talk about two villages that have developed around the two footbridges Ram Jhula and Lakshman Jhula.

It was my third visit to the place, where the Ganges River flows out of the Himalayan foothills. Arriving there, felt like coming home to me.

The other times I had been there with my daughter. I had stayed at a guesthouse, while doing a yoga course. This time, I would stay in the yogic environment of an Ashram. In the past, I had been to Swami Dharmananda's Yoga Philosophy classes in the Sri Ved Niketan Ashram and decided to stay there. This way I would also be able to attend the early morning meditations, guided by the Swami.

Things had changed since I last was there. Last time the classes had been given in one of the Swami's rooms, with a view through the entrance towards the Ganges. Now, they were held in the windowless but larger basement. Fans were used to move the mouldy smelling, humid air.

The Swami lit a few sticks of incense and circled them around the images of various Hindu Gods and master teachers before starting his class.

In a funny practical way, he taught us how to deal with different life situations as well as yoga, Vedanta and the Bhagavad Gita. The airless environment became secondary to the joy I felt listening to his wisdom.

To my own surprise, I knew the answers to many of his questions. I hadn't known that I knew—if this makes any sense. It was like an instantaneous knowing popping up from inside me. The less I thought, the clearer and faster the answers appeared. I just had to stay fully present.

The yogic philosophy and the different yoga practices were resonating with me in a way that felt just like *my path*.

One morning, the Swami was talking about the human need to give God a form. He said that it makes it easier for people to develop *a feeling* for what we call God. People can't relate on a personal level to the yogic concept of Higher Consciousness or Absolute Truth.

"The Buddhist believe system doesn't talk about God either, you see. So we Hindus just made Buddha a God!" he said humorously.

"I have my Krishna" he said, pointing to an image of the Hindu-God Krishna. There were three images of the Krishna: Baby-Krishna, Krishna as a beautiful young man with his flute and Krishna as an old wise man.

Then he asked us, "Who of you likes this Krishna?" pointing at the baby. Several middle-aged ladies raised their arm.

"Ah, you see, here are the mothers! And who likes this Krishna?" he said, pointing at the one with the flute. I was amongst the people raising their hand. He looked at each one of us. Then he said, "Here are the ones who look for a lover! And who likes this Krishna?" pointing at the third and last one. "Here are the ones who look for wisdom."

The Swami was giving people the chance to see him privately and get his advice. After class, I asked him for an appointment and he said I could meet him the next day in the afternoon.

I wasn't sure what I wanted to ask him. I had a more general wish of meeting him and—I guess—being seen by him. I was aware that we are unable to see our own shadow, and I was open to receive his directions or any insights into my personality, which I couldn't see. The next morning in class, the Swami was missing a group of students that had left for a tour to the source of the Ganges. He wasn't pleased with who had remained in class and I watched him asking his Krishna to send him more students.

When I went to meet him in the afternoon, the secretary told me that he couldn't see me right now. All of sudden, a large group of fifty Russians had turned up. They were making a documentary on yoga and were interviewing him.

I nearly burst out laughing. "Was this how Krishna had responded to his request?" The thought amused me so much I couldn't stop giggling, as I walked back into my room.

The gates of the ashram were open until ten at night and one could move freely in and out. It was kind of the easy version of ashram life. I enjoyed the freedom of choosing my own meals.

Passing all the beggars in the streets, made me very aware of the fact that I could just get any meal I desired. Several ashrams were serving food to the poor in the streets. No one had to starve in this holy town.

I kept to my rule and every day gave something to one person. Once, as I was enjoying a fresh orange juice from a street vendor, a beggar approached me and I ordered another juice for him. The same man kept asking me for food, whenever I passed him. He used to hold the fingers of his right hand together, moving it towards and away from his mouth. A little further down the street the ashram was just serving food to everyone hungry. I had no compassion for him. In some cases begging is just a bad habit.

*   *   *

One day, I went to the Sivananda Ashram on the other side of the river. There was no yoga class but there was a celebration going on. One of the elder Swamis had his birthday and there were three boats decorated with flower garlands to take people on a river cruise. Musical instruments and speakers were carried onto the boats. I was invited by one of the women to come along and happily jumped into the boat that carried only women.

Soon the party started with the singing of Kirtan. It sounded more like shouting than singing and was further distorted by the sound-system. One of the western swamis looked distressed by the noise coming out of the speakers. One has to note Indian parties are loud. As Greek festivities are quite similar, I was used to roaring speakers and loud singing out of tune that is all part of the fun.

After the boat ride, we all queued to receive a sweet and a little basket made of banana leaves that contained flowers and a candlelight. When the candle was lit, we placed it into the Ganges and watched all the lights being carried down the stream.

When I crossed the footbridge on the way back to my room, I heard a voice behind me asking me in English whether I knew the place. I turned around and looked at a tall blond guy, who seemed a little disorientated. He said he had just arrived. I didn't mind to showing him where the main market area with shops and restaurants was. He invited me for a drink that in a "holy place" is always non-alcoholic; just like the food is vegetarian only. I agreed but first I wanted to attend the "Ganga

Aarte", a ceremony for the Ganga with more harmonious chanting of mantras and prayers. It takes place every evening at the riverside temple of the Parmath Niketan Ashram. All the boys and swamis of this ashram gather around a ritual fire together with the many visitors to the open event.

He was impressed by the colourful crowd and the devotional singing of the little boys. When we had a drink of lemon soda, we told each other in brief our story. His name was Tim. He was English, travelling by himself on a motorbike. His journey was very different to mine, as he wasn't a spiritual seeker but more interested in the old British colonies. He wished India was still under British control. Soon I said good night. Our points of view and interests were very different.

The next evening, I bumped into him again at the Ganga Aarti. When we went for dinner together, he told me more about the life he'd left behind in England and I told him more about my life.

There were things he was telling me I could relate to and I started to feel friendlier towards him. The spicy dinner required a dessert and I knew where to go for that!

What is it about food that can create connection between people?

When I introduced him to the best apple samosa in town that we fully enjoyed together, Tim became my friend.

He said he was going on a trip up into the Himalayas to see the highest mountain peak in India and asked me, whether I wanted to join him. It sounded like a good adventure. I loved the idea of driving through the mountains on a motorbike and I had no doubts that he was a good and responsible driver. On the other hand, I was dedicating this period to yoga and the Swami had just asked me to sit in the first row in class what is quite an honour. I said I'd think about it.

Until the very last hour I couldn't decide what to do. Now, I really felt the need to talk to the Swami and ask for some advise. In some way I was probably asking for his permission.

I went to the office and asked if I could see him. I said it was important to me and told them that I had already had an appointment arranged with him that didn't happen.

"Ok" the secretary said. "I will try and phone Swamiji."

When he phoned him, the swami was just about to have his lunch. He still asked to talk to me on the phone. I apologized for disturbing him during his lunch hour and explained that I was having an inner conflict and needing his advice. Did my voice sound really troubled? To my surprise he agreed to see me right then.

After introducing myself, I mentioned the appointment that hadn't happened when Krishna had sent him all these Russian people for an interview.

"What do you mean?" he said, looking puzzled.

I explained that I had watched him asking Krishna for more students, and how amused I was with the way Krishna had responded to his request. He looked at me with his mouth open.

Then we came to the subject of my inner conflict. I told him about the invitation to the motorbike trip into the Himalayas. He replied, "That's good. What is the problem?"

I said, "I feel that I don't want to miss your class, especially after being called to sit at the front."

"Oh, I see" he said. "Do you want to go on this trip?"

"Yes!"

"You just go then! The class will still be here when you come back! Anything else?"

"No", I said and thanked him from my heart.

Happily, I left and quickly went to find Tim to tell him I was coming. My friend was nearly gone. He hadn't expected me to come anymore.

It took me ten minutes to pack my bag and off we went.

My heart was singing as we drove along the—up here turquoise—Ganges, the river that I adore, into the mountains that I also adore. I was so glad I had talked to the Swami. Otherwise, I would have carried feelings of guilt with me. Now, I could fully enjoy the ride. My body hadn't sat on a motorbike for years but to my great pleasure I felt it coping really well. It felt strong and flexible from all the yoga practice and easy to balance through all the bumps and curves of the road.

For Tim it was probably just another ride but to me it was something really special. Ladakh had been so dry like a mountain desert but these mountains were green. I loved it!

The intensive yoga practice must have made me very sensitive for energies too. As I sat closely behind Tim, I was surprised to feel an energy exchange happening between our chakras.

I wonder, what he perceived. At some stage he looked at me with astonishment and said: "You are so gentle!"

When the sun set behind the mountains, we started looking for a place to spend the night. There weren't many hotels around and it took us a while to find an acceptable room for an acceptable price. Some places looked really barracked and were still quite expensive.

I left all the negotiating to him because this is men's business in India.

It was already dark, when we finally found a hotel that was situated on a hillside and seemed nice. We had to decide whether to take a room together or not.

Tim said, he would be a gentleman and I said, I knew he would, otherwise I wouldn't have gone with him!

Officially though, we played husband and wife not to offend the Indian customs. The receptionist knew of course that it was a lie, when we gave him our passports for registration. Discretely, he ignored the lie and went with it like it was the truth, playing his part of the game.

Feeling like his sister, I slipped into the large bed next to Tim, as I had done many times before with other friends who happen to be men. He seemed to be a little tensed though and asked me if we could at least hug.

"Oh, oh . . ."—I felt alarmed. I reminded him of his gentleman talk and made it clear that it was alright with me, as long as he wouldn't try to go for more. I fell asleep, while he was softly stroking my arm.

The next morning, we saw that the hotel was overlooking a wide valley. A small town was spreading out through it. The mountain peaks draw a beautiful line on the horizon. We hadn't been able to see all this in the darkness last night. We probably had been too tired to pay much attention anyway.

Now, we were taking in the beautiful view, while we were waiting for our breakfast. We knew that in India it could take a while for the breakfast to be prepared. So we laid back and enjoyed the beautiful scenery. We knew that a long, hot journey was lying in front of us.

Finally, we were ready and back on the road. The sun was very strong at that altitude and together with the breeze of the ride quite dehydrating. On our way, we passed many mountain springs but we wouldn't risk drinking from them. Luckily, there were enough places along the road that sold water.

The breeze became colder the higher we got. In the end, it got really cold. We reached the ski resort in Auli. From here we would have a fine view of Nanda Devi, with its 7816m the highest mountain peak in India.

Tim wanted to check out the cabins first. To our disappointment they were cold, run down and not inviting at all. None of us wanted to stay there, which meant we were forced to drive back into the town Joshimath to find some accommodation.

We were shivering, as we headed back down the mountain.

Again, it took us a while to find an agreeable room. Tired and hungry we checked in and were soon back on the road, looking for a place to have dinner. This time, we walked along the street. It was safer to leave the bike in the car park of the hotel and we had been sitting on it all day anyway.

The chilly air was filled with fire smoke. In India, a lot of cooking is still done over open fire. We decided on a restaurant filled with locals. This was very different from touristy Rishikesh. We received interested looks and questions. The owner welcomed us effusively and made us feel very special. I must say, that that was quite comforting after the long, tiring journey.

Back in our hotel, it was cold enough to snuggle closely in bed. By now, our bodies were comfortably familiar with each other. Again he was softly stroking the skin of my body. It just felt so good. What should I say? While I was fully enjoying it, I slowly melted into a deep sleep.

When I woke up, he was still stroking my body. He hadn't been able to sleep all night, he told me. He had been too aroused, he said. Well, he had managed to turn my body on too!

For the reason of safe sex, we controlled our desire and continued our trip in an attempt to catch sight of Nanda Devi. The road led us into a long narrow valley that was surrounded by many high mountain peaks, but didn't seem to get us closer to the mountain we were heading for.

We saw a sign for a homestay at the beginning of a foot trek. The path went along a mountain, into a small gorge and looked beautifully inviting. We felt tempted to hike there and hide away for a couple of days, but we couldn't just leave the motorbike behind. We also had kind of arranged to stay the night in the same hotel where we had spent our first night. So we just started our return trip, without having caught a glimpse of the highest peak.

It was already late in the evening when we arrived at the hotel. This time the suite was available. We looked at each other, reading each other's mind. We knew what was going to happen this night. Tim decided to treat us to it.

He should have been exhausted after driving all day and a sleepless night. Instead, both of us felt charged with excitement. We had a royal dinner and spend the rest of the night finally surrendering ourselves to our bodies' desire and all the Kama Sutras we could think of. He took the role of the leader and I followed the guide.

Back in Rishikesh, we spend another sensual night in his hotel room together. Then I returned to my Spartan room in the ashram, feeling fulfilled by our little adventure together. He had become my English Gentleman and I had become his Golden Girl.

The next night we met for dinner. Afterwards, he walked me back to the ashram and we took a moment to sit down by the Ganges. Expressing our gratitude for the precious time we had together, we said goodbye to each other. He was ready to continue his journey and I to get back to my yogic life style.

Non-attachment is one of the main lessons in yoga. It is an on going process of receiving life and what it is gifting to us and then let it go again. The clinging is what creates the suffering. Everything and everyone that leaves us creates the space for something new to arrive.

Resisting this process had caused a lot of suffering for me in the past but slowly I seemed to get better at it.

I asked the guy who stayed in the room next to mine how the class was while I was away.

"You know, the Swami was talking about you" he said.

"What? Talking about me?"

"Yes! He talked about awareness and then he talked about you, saying this woman is aware."

"Oh, really?" I said surprised and also a bit delighted. I was happy to be back in the ashram and looking forward to the next class.

The next class though, didn't happen too soon. The Guru of the ashram was sent to hospital and the Swami was there to look after him. In class we had heard many stories of the Guru, who was now an old man. He had already lived far beyond anybody's expectations and predictions. Now, it looked like he was going to finally leave his body.

After speaking to my room neighbour, I turned around and who was coming down the aisle? The English gentleman!

He wanted to see some more of my smile, he said. As he was driving out of town, he had realized that and had turned around.

"Wow", I thought, "sometimes when we get over our own attachments we get to deal with the attachments of the others."

So there he was again. He even had managed to get back into the same hotel room. They were just cleaning it out when he got back. I was quite happy though, to stay in the ashram and things between us became more complicated, as they do when attachment and wanting comes in.

One night, we nearly got ourselves in trouble. We had been visiting some friends who stayed in a complex of guesthouses a little bit out of town. One of the guys I had already met on the roof of a bus, when visiting a monastery in Leh and again later in MacLeod Ganj during one of the open stage nights. We all felt very joyful. Wasn't it incredible how and under what circumstances we met again and again?

This is how it often goes when one travels in India.

As we were having a good time, while having dinner together, it got late. When Tim and I wanted to get back into town, there were no more rickshaws around. What could we do?

At that moment, a truck came along and we stopped it. We asked the driver for a ride back into town.

"Yes, yes" the driver smiled and waved us in. We soon realized, that he wasn't fully right in his mind. He was either drunken or drugged and his whole behaviour felt weird and dodgy. He stopped when a bike was lying in the middle of the road and my friend, wanting to be helpful, jumped out to remove it. Immediately the dodgy man grabbed my hand and started kissing it. I tried to pull it away from him, but he only let go of it when my friend returned into the truck. We got out of there as soon as possible, only to find that more dodgy looking creatures in the streets were making an attempt to follow us. That was a totally different place from the one I knew. The night had changed the village into a different place, with a reality that I hadn't encountered before, as I used to be back in the ashram early.

Luckily, a little further down the road we finally found a rickshaw to bring us back into the safety of Tim's hotel. The ashram gate had long closed.

*　　*　　*

There is another event that has stayed in my memory from the time I spent in Rishikesh. At some stage during my stay in the ashram, I was lying in bed and my heart went out to a baby that was crying somewhere in the neighbourhood. No one seemed to pay attention to the crying baby and its crying became more and more desperate. I felt its hunger and its need for the warm breast of the mother and the pain of being left alone. It resonated with the baby inside me and I felt the pain becoming nearly unbearable. This awoke a longing in me for changing that reality.

Reality? What is real and what isn't? Is there only one reality or are there many? Which reality is ours and how does it get created? When something gets created, can't we as well destroy it and create something different then? How?

During my training in craniosacral therapy, I had learned a technique that clears stuff from our cell memory by the use of three stages. In the first stage, called reposition, we go fully into the remembered experience with as much detail as we can, in order to bring up as much stored information as possible. Then we detach ourselves from the subjective experience, by stepping out of the "I" and looking at the situation from a distance. By doing so, we usually get a wider picture showing the surroundings and anyone involved and gain more understanding of the others and what made them act as they had. This stage is called deposition. Then in the third stage, called metaposition, we rewrite the whole story in an ideal way, just how it would ideally have been for us. This changes the energy of distress and suffering and creates the experience of peace, joy and contentment. Again, we can fill it with as much detail as we like to give it as much substance as possible. This is a way of healing any issue.

Here, with the crying baby, I sensed a mother that was occupied with other duties and unaware of her baby's needs. I fully indulged in the mental creation of a home with a protected yard, clean and with flowers, where a child was well nurtured and free to explore its little world. I indulged in the sweet joy of drinking milk from the mother's breast while being caressed and sung to. And as I, as a baby, grew older, I was nurtured by my loving family to develop all my talents.

I don't know if that did anything for the baby in the neighbourhood who had stopped crying by then. It certainly healed an old wound inside me. And wasn't my own healing part of my journey?

Time passed as I continued to go to different yoga teachers, exploring different styles and classes. Some teachers were quite rough with their students. I saw one of them stepping on peoples' thighs for a better stretch and decided to stick to Yogi Sundeep. In the past, I had already done a one-month course with him. In his classes I felt in the "right place". He's an angelic being and surrounded by an aura of "sweetness".

He also is a Reiki Master and from him I had received the First and Second Degree in Reiki, some years ago.

We both felt it was time for me to be initiated as a Reiki Master, which is usually a powerful experience. Due to the daily yoga and meditation practice my energy level was already quite high. What would I feel now?

It is truly impossible to describe what one experiences during an initiation process. All I can say is that it feels very "sacred".

Something strange happened afterwards though. As I walked home one of the street dogs that was sleeping in the sun, suddenly got up and licked my hand.

As I was treating myself with the master symbol for twenty-one days, a blissful sweet feeling settled in more and more and became how I used to feel. Still, there were moments when things upset and disturbed me, but that was more temporary now. The underlying basic feeling became that of swimming in the honey and I was willing to share!

I shared it with my neighbours in the ashram, people who sat next to me in the restaurant, the shopkeepers I dealt with, the cows in the streets, the beggars whose need felt real and I shared it with my friend Tim, the English gentleman.

One night, we were sitting on the roof terrace of a restaurant by the Ganges. He was feeling upset. He didn't get the beauty of giving love in freedom, without *needing*, without *wanting* something from anyone else. He talked about love and the meaning of partnership. In that moment, I suddenly knew deep in my heart, what the message had once, before my journey, revealed to me; there was a partner, a soul mate for me somewhere out there, but it wasn't him. In some corner of my mind I sensed New Zealand.

Maharani

What else did I want to see and experience in India before leaving the country?

It was my third trip to India and I still hadn't been to the Taj. Was now the time to finally visit it? I also wanted to visit 'my camel' in Rajasthan.

To tell the story of my camel, I need to go back in time, to my last journey around India. Two years earlier, I had been on a camel safari in the desert around Jaisalmer, "The Golden City". A guy from Belgium and I had booked the tour through our hotel. Early in the morning, when it was still dark we were picked up by a jeep and taken out to some small village in the desert, where three camels and a camel driver were already waiting for us. By the time we arrived the sun, was just rising and I looked at the most beautiful camel I'd ever seen. It was love at first sight.

I was led to another camel though. The beauty—with the name Johnnie—was ridden by the camel driver, whose skin was nearly black from the desert sun. He held our camels on long ropes, as we took off into the Thar Desert that contains some sort of low bush and farmland. I was quite amazed, when I suddenly saw some melons popping up in front of us that were growing in the barren land.

When we rested in the shade of a large tree during the hot hours, our guide told us his story. He had left his village for a job as a toilet cleaner in a hotel in town. This is the lowest of all jobs, but he managed to pick up some

English and when he knew enough to have some sort of conversation with the tourists, he became a guide for the camel safaris that the hotel organizes. When he told us how little they were paying him per month—probably to make us aware that tips were needed and expected—we realized that that was half of the money each of us had paid for one tour!

We were fantasizing that if he had his own camels he would be able to get himself out of this state of "paid slavery". Maybe if he started with one camel and was able to slowly save enough money to buy another camel, and then the next one, and in time slowly build up his own business?

"Yes" he smiled "but how do I get my first camel?"

"Hey, wouldn't that be an act of development aid to buy him the first camel?", we considered enthusiastically. At least then we knew where our money was going, instead of donating to an organisation where one never knows where the money goes!

"We could buy Johnnie!" our guide said with shiny eyes.

During the following night, I woke up and lay awake under the millions of stars of the desert sky, thinking about my life and the life of our camel guide. When I thought about buying him Johnnie, I saw a shooting star. I went on thinking about different things and when I came back to the thought of buying Johnnie I saw another shooting star. Was that coincidence or was the universe trying to tell me something here?

I did the maths and wasn't sure whether I would still have enough money to continue my travels with ease, but I could live on chai and chapati for a short while if it came to the worst and our guide needed his first camel!

"Hey, could we really buy Johnnie?" I asked him the next morning. He looked at me with eyes of excitement.

"You mean you want to buy Johnnie?"

"Yes!" I replied. He jumped and shouted with joy: "Mama, you're the camel boss!"

I said to him: "God gives you a chance!"

Since then, two years had passed and I had spoken to him on the phone several times. I booked a train ticket to Jaiselmer.

He was very excited when I said that I would come and go on a safari with him, on "my own camel"—as he called it—though it really was his. And I was excited to see how my little aid had developed.

I had told Tim the story of my last camel safari and he understood that I wanted to go there. By then, he had seen more than enough of Rishikesh. Several times he had made an attempt to get on with his own journey and was glad to finally do so.

We both were going to Haridwar first. I remembered that he had once mentioned how much he wanted to go to a cinema. Watching the Indian people living the movies is a theatre in itself!

I suggested we go together to the movies in Haridwar and spend the night there, before I would get on the train to Delhi. He liked the idea. We decided to make an attempt and see whether my suitcase would fit on his motorbike. Otherwise, I would take a rickshaw and meet him in Haridwar.

Leaving Rishikesh is always like leaving home to me and fills me with nostalgia. How long would it take me to get back there? One year? Two? Or even more?

The challenge to get myself and all my luggage onto the bike distracted me from nostalgic thinking. One arm over my suitcase and the other around my friend's chest, I tried to keep my balance on the windy, bumpy road. Here we were again, off into the next adventure!

When the sun went down, turning all the dust in the streets into an "orangy"-golden lit cloud, I was hit by a wave of ecstasy. How lucky was I to experience all this?

As usual, it took us a while until we had found and checked into a nice hotel. We were late and missed the famous Ganga Arte of Haridwar. When we arrived at the sacred site by the Ganges River, the evening ceremony of prayers and chanting was over and the crowds were gone. The later show in the cinema wouldn't start for a while and we had some time to bathe our feet in the Ganges and have dinner on its banks. I felt comfortably relaxed in my friend's presence. Alone, I would have been much more aware of *everything* going on around me.

When we entered the shabby looking cinema, we saw the major show had been the earlier one. The theatre was filled with litter that the crowd had left behind. Only a few visitors, mostly men, were in this show. The Bollywood movie was funny, romantic, tragic, musical and scary altogether, designed to push all the buttons of emotions in the viewer. It was about a haunted house, which intensified the already spooky atmosphere in the theatre. After the intermission the numbers of visitors had slightly increased. Half of them were stretched out for a sleep.

It wasn't exactly what we had imagined, but definitely an unforgettable experience!

The next morning we stood on the platform, waiting for the train to roll in.

"Can I invite you to a camel safari?", I asked my friend, when I kissed him goodbye.

In Delhi, I had half a day to wander around before my train to Jaiselmer was leaving. There was a queue at the Clerk room where I wanted to leave my luggage before visiting the market. As I was standing in the queue, I was hit by a sickening smell. Even the local people pulled their face in disgust. Soon I discovered the source of it. Not far away someone had left a nauseating smelly, mushy pile of shit behind.

I was quite used to the sight and smell of shit in India and not easily shocked, but this one was something else! The comical tragedy was that we couldn't just walk away from it, as we were forced to wait in the queue. So everyone was bearing the horrible fumes, and I had to laugh and choke at the same time.

With relief I checked-in my luggage and left for the market area. Outside the station I went to the prepaid taxi stand and bought a ticket that I would use later to get from the New Delhi Train Station to the one in Old Delhi. I also asked how long it would take to get there, so I had an idea how much time I had and wandered off to a beauty parlour for a foot-massage.

In the end, I nearly missed my train to Jaiselmer due to a traffic jam. My rickshaw driver tried desperately to find a way around the jammed streets, where nothing seemed to move. The thought of missing the train freaked me out, as it hadn't been easy to make my reservation for a bed in the sleeper carriage and there was only one train per day going there.

My whole neck and head went hard as a stone by the stress I felt. I prayed to the Hindu God Ganesha who is the remover of all obstacles for help. There was nothing I could do about the situation! I needed to relax! "Relaaaax", I remembered the Swami telling us in a singing voice in the yoga class. "Relaaax . . . relaaax . . . relaaax . . ." I kept telling myself in the same voice. Another prayer for God's help and I became a little calmer.

We arrived late at the station and my train should have left by now. My only hope was that the train was late too. I would do what I could and make a run to maybe catch it. This was the only time I made use of a porter, who luckily knew to which platform I needed to get and together we ran through the crowds in the station and got to the—empty—platform.

He looked at me with pity but there was a train on the other platform and—yes—we were told it is the train to Jaiselmer. The porter had made a mistake!

Out of breath we found the right carriage and reached my seat. Thanks to the porter! Thanks to Ganesha! I got my train!

I hadn't got quite over the stress of getting the train, when the next stress followed. As the train rolled out of Delhi, the carriage filled up with men that squeezed themselves into every little corner left. I had the upper bed but that didn't stop them from squeezing in next to me. A claustrophobic wave hit me and I chased everybody of my bed. Two of the Indian 'proper' passengers supported my attempt and made sure no one else would climb on it again. After leaving Delhi behind the train got less crowded anyway. During the night I was only disturbed by the passing chai-wallah. I was used to the on going shout of chai-chai-chai from other train journeys and managed to get some sleep, a small bag with all my valuables next to me in my sleeping bag. My daypack I kept by my head while my suitcase was chained to the lower seat.

The last part of the journey was hot and dusty. The carriage had no closing windows and the sand blew right into it.

When the train reached Jaiselmer it was early afternoon and I stepped out into the heat.

No signs of my camel guide Ismael who was supposed to pick me up. In need of a shadier spot I walked into the station building and phoned him.

He said, "Go to taxi stand!"

Then, I saw him at the other side of the road, as he was talking into his cell phone and wondered, "What's this? Doesn't he recognize me anymore?"

I went to him but instead of greeting me, he started walking and gave me a short look to see if I was following. He got into one of the last rickshaws in the long queue and gave me a sign to follow. He treated me like a stranger; totally different from how he had talked to me on the phone. It all felt weird and his whole behaviour didn't make any sense to me.

When I asked where we were going, he said to a friend's house. We reached a neighbourhood on the foot of the Old Fort and the taxi stopped. I paid the rickshaw driver and Ismael unlocked a large wooden door that led into an inner courtyard. When the door closed behind us, his face changed into a big smile. He stretched his arms towards me, "Mama! Welcome, welcome! Now we can talk!"

I looked puzzled and he explained to me, that with his clothes he is not allowed to enter the station and talk to tourists. Only business people could do that. I realized that his clothes showed, that he belonged to the lower caste of labourers. It dawned on me, that he must have been afraid to get himself into trouble by talking to me. So he made it look like we just happened to walk in the same direction. How unaware I was about the social input of the caste system!

He told me to have a seat, while he would make some tea. We exchanged our news and talked about the camel safari. I told him that I needed to make a phone call and see whether a friend of mine was coming too. I asked him if he had bought another camel by now and he said no, one of his children had been sick and he had spent a lot of money on doctors and medicine. Truth? Or tall tale? Who knows?

I saw in Ismael's face that he didn't like the idea of someone else joining us. I made several attempts and finally reached Tim. It was all a bit crazy, he said, but he was on a long drive through the desert and all just to get some more of my smile! He'd probably be there before sunset.

"Great!" I said with joy. "Call me when you're here and I'll meet you by the big lake and water reservoir Gadi Sagar!"

We would need another camel now and more food which all needed to be organized. I left Ismael with money for the food shopping and wandered leisurely to the lake for a boat ride, as I had plenty of time. We agreed to leave town by night, once my friend arrived and then sleep outside in the desert.

The English gentleman reached the Golden City shortly after sunset and looked exhausted from the long trip. We still needed to look for a safe place where his bike could be stored and he was desperate for a shower. We found a hotel that covered both and went back to the house where I had left Ismael. Next to it was a tiny shed where a young guy had already prepared dinner for us. It was a simple meal but we were so hungry, that we ate it gratefully. Finally, we were ready for the drive out into the desert.

Ismael had organized the additional camels that were brought to the water tank where we got off the jeep. We would sleep on the flat cistern, he said. I was excited to see Johnnie, but only got sight of his silhouette in the moonlight. Mattresses were rolled out and we finally could stretch out, relax and gaze into the night sky. I was glad, that Tim was with us.

The safari was pretty much a repetition of the one I had done two years ago. I enjoyed the rhythmic swing of the camel ride, and I loved how my mind rests in the empty space of the desert.

Tim looked content too. I had tied a cloth around his head, which made him look like Lawrence of Arabia. His face had totally relaxed and he looked like he had melted onto his camel. Ismael sang songs of the desert, as we rode along.

During the hot hours of the day, we rested under the same tree, where we had rested two years ago. Here, the Belgian traveller and I had had the idea of buying a camel for our guide.

Like then, Ismael cooked lunch for us over the fire. He had a small pan for the chapatis and pots for rice and curry. He was a good cook. It was all tasty and everybody was happy.

In the afternoon, we stopped at a lake where the camels could drink water, and we could wash the dust and sweat of our faces and arms. Tim wanted to have a shower and left with a bucket for a bush. A little later, we heard him screaming and saw him jumping around. He had left his pants, hanging on a tree, and they were now full of ants.

Before sunset, we reached the same sand dune, where I had once been lying awake under the shooting stars, and decided to buy our guide his own camel. Had that changed anything in his life? It didn't seem so. He still worked for the same hotel and asked me not to tell them, that he was doing a safari with me, because that could cost him his job. He let us know what else he needed money for, and I made him understand, that I had nothing more to give. It was up to him to make use of his gift and see how that could earn him more money. I realized that he, coming from the farmer's caste, did not have a business mind.

My friend said to him, that a man had to use every opportunity and make something out of his life. But what did we know about his culture and how much opportunity for change the caste system allows someone to have.

It is still possible though, that an act of generosity changes someone's life. I know another case where someone bought a rickshaw for his driver, who had only rented it. The grateful driver, who then had become a rickshaw owner said, "You have changed my life, the life of my children and the life of my grandchildren!"

This didn't seem to be the case with my camel guide, though he'd become a camel owner.

We still had some ideas for the future. We talked about the possibility, that I'd bring a small group of friends with me for the next camel safari, and he would organize it.

After the tour, we invited him to have lunch with us in town. Tim gave him a good tip, and we wished him good luck for his life that was so different from ours and followed its own destiny. Still I'll always feel a connection to him through the camel Johnnie.

*   *   *

Back in the 'Golden City', my friend and I looked for a hotel in the old fort, with its ancient, story telling walls. Once again, we changed our roles and now played maharaja and maharani. We found a room that looked like it came out of a 1001-night-fairy tale, with its rounded and playful shaped windows, inner walls and pillars. The floor and bed were covered with colourful cushions and the bedcovers were ornately embroidered.

In its privacy we were free again to please each other and our bodies with all the Kama Sutras we felt inspired to. Timeless moments of intimate play carried us into bliss and ecstasy.

When the sun set and threw its golden light into our oriental chamber, we got up and watched it disappearing behind the Jain Temples. We saw, that the wall of the house opposite to ours was covered with small bats. There must have been a hundred of them! Soon they would take off for their night flight. We decided to get out of our chamber too and swarm into the night. We were feeling ravenously hungry.

Some of the restaurants have their tables right on the city wall. Here we were dining on cushions around a low table, with the view over the lights of the fort-surrounding town.

As we were served with courses of delicious food, my friend said, "Only the music is missing!"

And truth—we struggled to believe it ourselves—a musician showed up, sat down in front of our table, and asked if he could play for us.

It seemed like we could have anything we desired, just as a maharaja and maharani can. It was like having visible and invisible servants around us, delivering to us whatever we wanted.

It was not only our money that, once changed into rupees, had become so plentiful to allow that, it was also us, choosing it and allowing it to happen by stepping into—what we thought to be—the reality of a king and queen. To feel like a king is an inner attitude that doesn't depend on how much money one carries around in one's pocket, or on how big the castle is.

Tim told me about his stay in an old castle in the region of Shekhawati. He had spent some days of his journey there and had loved the place. To him the castle had become very special and he considered taking me there.

"And my wish to visit the Taj Mahal before leaving India? Should I leave it once again for another time?" I thought.

"Should we do the long drive through the desert on his bike together?"

Once again, we managed to get my suitcase, together with all of Tim's luggage on his bike and off we went. It was a one-day-drive on a long and straight desert road. Despite the sun, it all went well and with the very last light of the day we reached the old castle.

Tim had already phoned the owner of the hotel and had arranged for us to have a nice room. During his first visit, he had developed a good relationship with the prince, who was one of several princes and owners of the large old castle.

The room we were shown had its own terrace. The walls were decorated with fresco-like paintings that are characteristic for the region. It was large and its height extended into the gallery of another floor. Later we found out, that it actually was the room of the princess that she had emptied for us to stay!

I know, that sounds really fantastic and everyone would expect me to be full of delight with all this, but the opposite was the case. From the moment I stepped into this room, I had a weird feeling. I looked at the upper gallery and thought of ghosts, moving along the corridor. I basically didn't want to stay there and suggested to have a look at another room.

My friend, who had invited me to be there with him, wanted it to be really special and rejected the more ordinary and smaller room that I liked. He chose the majestic one and I accepted his choice, though I felt not happy with that. I could not get rid of the feeling that we were not alone in there, and felt very much reminded of the movie we had seen in the spooky cinema.

It caused tension between us because I couldn't feel how my friend expected me to feel: happy and delighted. That made him feel disappointed and angry with me. The next day, I started to feel unwell.

We still tried to make the best out of our stay and had some beautiful moments. We visited the traditional 'havelis' in town, as the ornately decorated buildings and residences are called. We were shown around the private quarters of the castle by the prince, and got to see some secret spaces in the old castle. We got to see a hidden interior hall and dining room that once upon a time was used during war times. Some parts were well maintained, while others looked run down and beaten by the weather.

We enjoyed excellent meals there, but I continued to feel unwell. My temperature was abnormal, as if my body was trying to fight something off. I didn't feel quite myself. I needed to organize my trip to the airport in Delhi, from where I would fly to my next destination, Bali.

The prince told us that one of the other guests, whom I had already met during dinner, would go to Delhi by taxi on the same day, and it may be arranged that I go with him.

How did I get so lucky? The man agreed to let me travel with him, but prepared me that it would take much longer, because he wanted to photograph along the way, and would travel on smaller roads. It still was going to work out for me, as my flight was leaving in the evening, and I was glad to avoid the local transport.

This time, the goodbye for the English gentleman and me would be a final one. The princess said to me, that when my friend would visit there again, she hoped I would be with him. What she meant was, that she wished for him and me to stay together.

Who knows, would there be another adventure for us to share—sometime and somewhere—in the future? Who knows?

The trip to Delhi that was not far away, took a long time, but was interesting. My host was on a photography journey, and had hired a taxi and a driver especially for this purpose, so he could stop whenever and wherever he wanted to take a picture. He had already published a photography book of India.

I sat in the front seat of the taxi and got to see a lot of hidden sites. The photographer needed the whole backseat for his equipment and himself. I was glad, I could just sit in a protected space the whole day, because my body was hurting and I felt physically awful. What was it that I hosted in my body?

The photographer was going to stay in a hotel quite close to the airport, and was so kind to take me right to the airport. I thanked him many times.

I slept through the whole flight to Bali, treated myself a taxi to Ubud, found a room in a homestay and fell into a delirious feverish sleep.

Bathed in sweat I woke up several times, went to the toilet, changed my shirt and fell asleep again. During the night I heard a roaring thunder so loud, I thought that one of the volcanoes was erupting. A heavy storm went on through the whole night.

When I woke up in the morning, the storm and my head had cleared. I had slept for a day and a night. Whatever I had carried in my body was gone. The fever was gone and I stepped outside into a sunny morning, hungry for some breakfast.

*   *   *

Butterfly Wings

*T*he air felt warm and humid. On the low table on my veranda, a thermos filled with hot water, instant coffee, sugar and tea bags were already waiting for me. How great was that?

Still feeling a bit weak, I made myself a tea and sat down on the small bamboo couch to take in my new environment. From my veranda on the first floor, I looked down on the roofs and gardens of the few houses in the neighbourhood and amongst them lush green rice fields, palms and other large tropical trees. It all looked very neat. I loved it.

"Good morning", I heard a friendly voice greeting me. I looked around into the smiling face of the guy, who had first shown me my room.

"Do you like breakfast? Do you like pancake?"

"Yes, please!" I answered enthusiastically and soon he came back with a plate of tropical fruits and a banana pancake. How great was that again? I didn't even have to go anywhere for my breakfast—it came to me! And the young Balinese was so light and kind and gentle! It was his *lightness* that impressed me mostly. That was so different from India!

I had a look at my room. It was bright and clean. Should I just be content with it and stay here? Or should I go for something better? What was the best? A hut came into my mind. Yes, I much preferred to stay in a hut!

After breakfast, I went out to have a look around and see, where I would find the right hut for me to stay.

"Transport? Do you need transport?" I was asked again and again, as I walked through the streets of Ubud. I had a look at many different places, most of them were over my budget, and finally found a group of bungalows, set in a beautiful garden, next to the landlord's own private temple, that were both: beautiful and affordable. One of them looked like "the right one" for me.

After the accommodation was sorted, I had a look around at what else the place had to offer. There was a yoga centre that offered many different classes and yoga styles. I felt, I had been to so many yoga classes in India—here I wanted to experience something different. I saw an announcement for an event to save the orangutans that got my attention. I checked the date and saw it was on this night. So I went there on that night, and watched a film about life in the rainforest and the wood industry that destroys it. The French filmmaker tried to show the environment from the eyes of an orangutan, who looks at everything in detail. In this way, the beauty of the forest was captured nicely by the filmmaker.

The audience was an international blend of tourists and expats. Our money would support the organization that aimed at raising awareness, also amongst the locals.

The expats seemed to have their own community in Ubud. Many of them run a business. One lady just opened a spa. It was announced that she had to give two hundred Thai free massage treatments in order to get her licence, and she was looking for people to work on.

This is how I got to be so lucky to receive a Thai massage almost every day for as long as I stayed in Ubud. I had been in the right place at the right time to hear about this. I also had given around two hundred free sessions, during the period of my craniosacral therapy training. Now, I was happy and grateful to be in the role of the receiver. The spa was beautiful, just like paradise and I felt truly very lucky.

Every morning, I would wake up and find a thermos with hot water for tea or coffee waiting for me. I usually had a two hours yoga session, doing my own practice, before breakfast. Similar to the homestay, where I had spent the first night, the breakfast—fruits and pancake—was served on my little veranda.

I remembered the dream that I once had, where the doctor had prescribed a journey to the most beautiful places on Earth. Now, I was really experiencing this journey. At that time, I nearly developed a cancer in the region of my root chakra, which is connected to the earth element. In the past, I often lacked a will for survival, which is also related to the same chakra. I was aware, that I struggled with life on Earth and in a body.

Once during a craniosacral session, I had an experience where I was floating as pure soul through space. I had felt so free and in bliss that I didn't want to come back into my body with all its limitations. Life on Earth had so many rules and society had so many laws and restrictions, that it was not fun to me. I realized, that I much preferred to be in the state of *pure soul*, which from a human perspective is death.

Surgery had done one part of the job towards healing, but what if I really didn't want be here? All my life I've had a kind of longing for death. It dawned on me that in order to stay alive, I needed to *deeply fall in love with life on Earth!*

Was that the true meaning of this journey? Yes, I could see this.

From now on, I would allow myself to fall more and more in love with all the beauty the Earth had to offer.

In Bali, I was in a good place for this. Apart from its natural beauty, Ubud is the cultural centre of Bali:

traditional dance and music performances are on every night.

One day, I hired a scooter to explore more of the island. As I'm not used to driving scooters, I scared a few people in the first corner, but then I got better. In Greece, bad drivers are called *dimosios kindinos,* which means public danger. After an hour, no one seemed to be aware of the public danger anymore and I enjoyed the ride through the countryside along rice terraces and small villages. My destination was the temple Pura Luhur Batukau on Bali's second-highest volcanic mountain. From there, I went onto one of the volcanic lakes and on my way back I visited several craft shops. I was on a mission to buy a Buddha statue for my brother. In the end, I drove around for seven hours and was pleased, I returned safely back from my little adventure.

There was another temple that I wanted to visit. It was built around Bali's holiest and largest fresh water spring. It is much closer to Ubud and I considered hiring a pushbike, to make it a different experience. I went to a travel agent and asked, whether it was easy to reach the temple by bike. It can be tricky to ask the locals in this way.

The agent answered, "Yes, you can. It's close!"

So I hired a pushbike but when I asked someone else for directions to Pura Ulun Danu Batur, the person looked doubtfully at the bike, saying it was very far!

To me, it became the experience of both parallels. The tour *to* the temple was very far and it became a long uphill ride. The Indonesian pilgrims cheered, when they saw me on the bike and by the time I finally reached the temple, I was nearly *famous.* On the way, many of the visitors had seen me and spoke to me, now.

I followed the queues of local devotees into the water basin at the spring, to receive the blessings of the

Goddess and to purify myself from feelings of sadness and jealousy.

The day before, I had received an email from Jason in New Zealand, saying that he had a partner, now. He was asking me, whether I was going to come for a visit, when I reached New Zealand—though things would be a little different, now. What should I say? I couldn't deny that through all my different adventures, I had held a tiny little flame of hope in my heart, that one day I would lie in his arms again. Now, the little flame had blown out and left a dark gap behind. That was the other reason for my bike ride: I tried to burn and wash this dark spot away.

The drive down *from* the temple back to Ubud was much shorter and the only challenge here was speed control.

At the end of the day, I felt somehow purified, still not totally, but the long yoga session, I had then, helped.

*   *   *

With all its temples, there is a strong religious feel to Bali. Bali is the only Hindu island in a mainly Islamic Indonesia. The spiritual feeling I got in India was transcendental while Bali felt *magical* to me.

Every day, I explored a different part of town. Sometimes, I had a conversation with other tourists but I was mainly on my own.

In Greece, I had suggested to my partner to meet me in Bali and have a holiday together to reconnect. When I spoke to him on the phone, it became clear, that he was in a very different mind-set and had other goals.

All along the journey, there had been moments when I missed him. It was fine and exciting to be on my own journey. Still, I sometimes missed him.

On one of those days, I called my partner in Greece. His voice was very heavy. I felt the heaviness on me, as I had often done before. It had been part of "my job" to help him carry his burden. One day, I reached a point, where I decided not to carry anyone else's burden anymore. If they wanted, I could show them how to let go of their burden, or at least get rid of some of their stuff, so the package would get a little lighter.

My own life had become much lighter since then!

Now, I felt the same old heaviness lingering over me and once again refused to take it.

I felt, I had just got wings to fly and was having a miraculous flight around the world. My wings though, were like butterfly-wings. They were just unfolding in all their beautiful colours and transparency and they were fragile. They would break if I tried to take on such a weight!

In all respect, I needed to let my partner carry his heavy stuff alone. It belonged to him. If it was mine, I wouldn't be able to get away from it even if I tried. Wanting to take someone else's cross also means, considering them too *weak* to carry it themselves.

I better protect my beautiful wings and keep flying, even if I had to do it alone, right now.

Would I, one day, find another butterfly?

I remembered one of my friends. She too, was like a butterfly and I started to write her a letter: "Dear butterfly sister . . . ."

*   *   *

Wanting to hug
an elephant

I wasn't always "swimming in the honey". There were moments when I felt lonely. On those days the barking dogs of Ubud that came running out from their owner's yard onto the street seemed to be more threatening and made me feel very vulnerable.

Instead of letting myself being carried away into a "down mood", I kept thinking "the best".

What was the best I could choose right now? After all, it's our own choice which road we take at any moment in our life. It's us who are in charge. That's what is meant by 'taking the highest responsibility for ourselves', as Greta had called it.

Every day can unfold as a new adventure when we are open to the existing possibilities.

This is what happened when I woke up one morning, feeling a little bit melancholic and empty inside. I tuned into my heart and asked: "What would you like to do today?"

For a moment there was silence, then I heard a voice inside me saying: "I would like to hug an elephant!"

"Hug an elephant?" I was surprised. Then I remembered that there was an elephant park not very far from here. I had seen a flyer, offering tourists a tour to the park with a pick up bus service from the hotel early in the morning. This was definitely not the way I wanted to do it!

After a short yoga practice and the usual pancake and tropical fruit breakfast, I went into a small office, down the road and asked the man in there, how I could get to the elephant park. He started to tell me about the tour and I let him know, I was looking for a different way. He thought for a while.

Then he said, "I can take you on the scooter when I finish work here." The money he wanted was less than what I would have paid, if I hired a scooter for a day. Happily I agreed.

Early in the afternoon, I found myself on the back of a scooter and driving through the countryside with the Balinese man. We passed areas where I hadn't been before and I could just relax and have a look around. When we reached the park he said, "You can take your time while I wait for you."

Inside, the elephants were doing a show for the tourists. It was the last one of the day and to my surprise the elephants seemed quite happy as they were doing it. We were told that these elephants had been rescued from Sumatra after the rainforest had been destroyed and they had lost their home. We were further informed that these were the smallest and friendliest elephants in the world.

After the show, the last tourist busses left and few people remained in the park. One of the guards showed me where I could get close to the elephants and feed them with chopped wood. Here, I could go really close to them and touch and stroke them. I was amazed how gentle the boys were with the elephants. The boys and the elephants all looked friendly and seemed to be smiling.

Yes, it's true, the boys were smiling and the elephants were smiling too!

I had never seen smiling elephants before! One of the boys showed me how to throw piece of wood into the elephant's mouth. She caught it, enjoyed it, and waited for the next piece. I threw another one . . . and another one . . . and another one. We both had so much fun and I felt like a child again, not getting tired of the repetition, and she didn't get tired of eating!

The boy showed me how I could place the wood right into her mouth and when I did, I touched the softest tongue I had ever touched in my life. Amazing that a wood-eating animal could have such a soft tongue! She was so gentle and I was so full of joy that I hugged her!

So there I was, happy, happy, happy, and hugging an elephant!

Then, it was time for the elephants to have their bath. They had finished their work for the day and were all led into the large pool for a bath.

I sat and watched them playing with each other, stroking one another with their trunks, rubbing their heads on each other, splashing water over each other, tickling the other with their trunk—it was absolutely beautiful to watch!

When they had enough they simply all gathered to leave and I had to leave too. The park closed for the visitors. I and another couple had been the only ones still in the park.

*　　*　　*

Before I went on my journey, a friend in Greece, who came regularly to Bali, had told me about two places I should visit. Ubud was the one and the other was Amed in the east of the island.

In India, one of the travellers I hung out with had told me that he had done a diving course in Amed. To learn how to dive had been one of my dreams for many, many years. Both of them had recommended the "Good Karma"

Bamboo Cottages for a stay. So this was my next travel destination.

I organised the journey what was easy. Many tour operators offered bus trips to Amed with a stop over in Padang Bai.

In the end it took quite a long time to get there. It was late afternoon when I finally arrived and the Good Karma Bungalows were about 8 km out of town. I looked around and now when I really needed "transport" there was no one around offering it.

I finally found some guys who had a small scooter. With a little effort one of them managed to get me and the suitcase on it. When the road went uphill the scooter became slower and slower. We laughed when I finally had to get off and walk. Apart from this the little scooter did well and got me to my next home.

A sign on the road said: "Talking and Joking with BABA—GOOD KARMA—Bungalows & Restaurant".

I looked down onto a small bay and the thatched roofs of several cottages, protruding among the trees and hoped that one of them would soon be mine.

I was lucky. One of the large cottages was free and because I was alone and it was low season, I got it for the same price of a small cottage.

How could it get any better than this?

The cottages were right by the beach and, after three month away from Greece, at last I was by the ocean again! The ocean . . . I don't know what it is but something connects me deeply to it.

I love the ocean—always have. My mother had told me that when I saw the sea for the first time in my life, I screamed in great joy. I was one year old and she had taken me to the beach during a holiday. She said that I didn't want to leave it again and cried desperately when she had carried me away.

Like a fish, I feel best in the water, looking at the other fish and swimming amongst them. I feel somehow at home under water. That's why I longed for learning to scuba dive.

For the moment though, I was happy to stay in my cottage on the beach and drift along in the water whenever I wanted.

The rest of my time, I did an extended yoga practice in the peace of my cottage. It was like moving in between the inner and the outer ocean. I was in bliss. I had everything I needed to be totally happy.

The restaurant was serving food all day long and I didn't need to worry about food. It was just there, ready. Whenever I felt hungry I could eat and be amongst people.

I hadn't met "Baba" yet. He seemed to be away and I was so "full" in my own company anyway that I didn't miss any talking and joking. Some of the guests were absolutely nice and interesting to talk to. Still I usually didn't hang out there for long.

One day, I was invited by one of the guests to join him and his friends on a walk up the river to a waterfall.

It sounded beautiful but I was in the middle of my yoga practice, when he appeared at my hut, and didn't want to go anywhere. He said that I could join them for dinner later, if I wanted, and I said that I might.

Later, I found myself in such a state of bliss that I never left the cottage. I don't know if I ever before had felt so devoted during my practice.

As I moved from posture to posture with my eyes closed, I saw light streaming into me. I had a powerful experience of energy and light filling different parts of my body until my whole field was vibrating and I had expanded far beyond the boundaries of my physical body. Was I light or was I bathed in light? I didn't know. I hardly knew where I was and for how long I stayed, where ever I was. After a while, I moved my blissful body into bed and drifted into a deep sleep.

I still think of that cottage and the blissful days I spent there. I had felt I could live there for the rest of my life, in simplicity, dedicated to my spiritual practice. Still—my journey wasn't over yet . . .

Life goes on and even the most blissful spiritual experiences have a return into "normal" life.

*　　*　　*

Bubbles in Blue

*A*t some stage, the time felt right to leave my cottage and do some investigations about a diving course.

Outside I met a group of people that were just leaving and could give me a ride to a diving school. I love the way synchronicity happens!

The man, who had asked me to join them for a walk, drove the car and we finally got to talk to each other.

He told me, he lived in Kuta and had just come to Amed for the weekend to spend some time with his daughter.

Once, I had overheard a conversation he'd had with her in the restaurant. I had happened to sit on the table next to them. I had had the impression that he was a father trying to approach his teenaged daughter who obviously had started to drift away from him.

Remembering how I myself had been through all the difficulties parents have with their adolescent kids, I had sympathized with him.

When I talked to him now, he seemed really nice and I noticed something like a sweet connection between us. Now, I wished I had talked to him earlier. He happened to know the owner of the diving school and when he dropped me off, he made sure they would look after me. Before he left, he gave me his business card and told me to look him up when I'd come to Kuta.

Two days later, I moved into one of the little bamboo huts that belonged to the diving school for the diving course.

I was pretty excited. Together with me there were two other "girls", one from England and one from Canada. The teacher and his assistant were from Belgium and France. They were "the boys" which created a playful dynamic in the group and we would have a lot of fun together during the following days.

First we, the girls, had to overcome some fears before we were able to get into the deeper water. On our way to the sea we met some other divers who had just come back from their dive.

"How was it?" we asked all excited "and what did you see?"

"Oh it was great. We saw a small shark!"

"Shark?" We looked at each other and none of us could share their enthusiasm. We became aware of the fact that divers are keen to see sharks, while we beginners hoped to stay as far away from them as possible. The word shark triggered a deep-rooted fear in us!

In our first lesson we needed to do some exercises with all our diving gear in 3 m depth. I wasn't used to breathe under water and panicked, at first. Once my nervous system checked that there was oxygen supply under water my body relaxed and I was fine.

One of the other girls struggled more. She made several attempts to get down but shot up in panic every time. I sent her Reiki to make it easier for her and soon she was with us.

We learned the sign-language of the divers in order to talk to each other under water and let everyone know that we're ok or not.

Everything was done in slow motion. The way our teacher applauded us in slow motion, when we did well with our tasks, made me laugh and hundreds of bubbles came out of my mouth, what made me even more laugh and the world around me filled up with bubbles!

When all of us were ok and knew how to behave, we started our first little under water trip. In slow motion we drifted into the miraculous under water world of silence. Colourful fish were looking at us while we were adoring them.

All smiles and shiny eyes, we came back from our first diving experience.

During the following three days we had two dives around and through an old shipwreck. The lack of good visibility turned it into a slightly spooky experience, which was even more exhilarating.

We saw a whole forest of soft and hard corals. We got to meet angelfish and parrotfish and many, many other colourful fish.

On one occasion, our instructor was attacked by a triggerfish. He had to kick it away with his flippers. Later, he told us that that hadn't been the first time and how he hated the triggerfish for that. The fish isn't very big but can get quite aggressive and bite real chunks out of people. At Good Karma I had seen a guy whose ear had been ripped badly by the fish.

One of our buoyancy exercises took a funny turn when our instructor suddenly went into a meditation posture. We, the girls, looked at each other, laughed and tried to keep a serious face while we copied him. His assistant suddenly looked at a circle of floating meditators. Then the instructor went into headstand—and we after him. Then he did a somersault—and we after him. His assistant was watching the circus from the side, not believing it.

Yes, we had fun together! When diving one's buddies become as important as oneself. We had to be aware and look after each other at all times. That's the law. Thus we developed a strong sense for the team that we were. After our dives it seemed natural to go out for dinner and spend our evenings together. There was a deeper connectedness in this group than what I had felt in other groups on my travels. And still—after three days it was all over and each of us girls went our own way, again.

A diver now, I returned to the Good Karma Cottages and spent another set of peaceful days there. Every day one of the local ladies came to my cottage, asking if I wanted a massage and sometimes I let them massage me, just to give them some business.

I too had thought of offering massages to the other guests but these ladies needed to feed their kids at home and I didn't want to interfere with their business.

When it was time to leave, I phoned the man who had given me his business card and told him that I was coming to Kuta. He was just leaving for Singapore. He said that he would be back after three days and that he would be happy to see me then.

Once again, I was lucky to get a ride, this time with an Indonesian couple from Jakarta on honeymoon. They were very sweet people. We stopped for some sightseeing on the way and reached Kuta in the late afternoon. I found a hotel in the touristy party area of town, made myself at home and went out for dinner.

I felt tired after the long day and the journey and thought to have a quick meal and an ice-cold beer and soon go to bed.

Friends had said to me, "Don't go to Kuta. It's full of tourists! It's full of drunken Australians! It's awful!" and here I was right in the middle of it!

To my own surprise it didn't annoy me at all. After all the "quiet time" I was enjoying it!

I like the many-fold ways of life and during this journey I was enjoying the different qualities each place had to offer. Here it was: "Let's party!"

As I sipped on my beer, I relaxed into the busy feel of the place. The restaurant where I was having my dinner had a life music night. Two guys on a guitar were playing popular rock and reggae songs. They saw that I was alone and that I was actually listening to them while other guests were busy talking. So they started to say things through the microphone to me, which drew some attention to me.

Soon, a guy from Germany came to my table and asked, if he could join me. While I was talking to him, another guy, who was walking down the street, gave me a look. Our eyes met and, I don't know why, I had to look at him for a second time.

He seemed somehow familiar to me. As he walked by, I had a third look at him because I really thought, I knew him from somewhere. He turned around and he also looked at me again. It was strange and the guy at my table noticed it, too.

The music had got me into a nice space and suddenly I wasn't tired anymore! When the musicians stopped playing, I was up for party!

My new German friend had been in Kuta for a while and introduced me to the nightlife of the place. Soon I found myself on the dance floor amongst many people much younger than me. Some looked as if they had come straight from the surfboard into the club. I saw middle-aged tourists with young Indonesian women sitting around in silence. It was quite obvious what was going on here. They couldn't communicate with each other and many of them looked bored.

At some stage, I lost the German guy somewhere in the crowd and started to feel bored myself. The music was not my music. The people were not my kind of people. I went to the bathroom and was ready to leave, when I bumped into the guy, that I had seen earlier, and with whom I had had this strange look-exchange.

We looked at each other with surprise and he invited me for a drink. We tried to talk but had to scream into each other's ears. So we went outside and sat down by a fishpond. I can't remember what we talked about, just that our conversation felt so natural like we had been friends for years.

He had the great idea to have a swim in the pool at his hotel and I felt so easy with him that I agreed. I was so glad to cool down in the mellow water that I was not thinking. He took me by surprise, when he suddenly grasped me and swirled me around. The last thing I was looking for was a sort of one-night-stand.

Still, he made me dizzy in a very sweet way and I suddenly felt thirsty for "another glass of water", as my Greek partner would have called it.

During the rest of the night that we spent together in his hotel room, I again had this strange feeling that I knew him. I just *knew* that I knew him and I felt that I loved him. It was truly weird! Beautifully weird!

The Greeks have a saying: "Mysterious are the paths of the heart." I looked at the guy who wasn't particularly handsome—not that he was ugly—and, for reasons I didn't understand, had triggered the love in my heart. I thought of Tim who was really good-looking and despite all his efforts hadn't been able to move my heart in this way.

In this moment, I became aware of the stupidity of choosing a partner by his looks. What's the value of having a partner with a pretty face and a "shity" character? He (or she) will only make us suffer! (In my life I've had a taste of this!) And how often do we turn away someone with a beautiful wide-open heart, who could give us "heaven on earth" just because we don't like his nose, maybe. Did that make any sense?

The next morning, as we sat side by side in his bed, talking like old friends, he looked at me and with an expression of surprise he said: "I like you!"

We were given little time together. He was flying out on the same day to Thailand.

It felt nearly unfair but, I suppose, that's how it had to be.

He soon needed to get ready for his trip and pack, and I went back to my own hotel room. He insisted to meet me later for lunch and so I saw him one more time.

He convinced me to move into a better hotel, one that had a swimming pool, and I promised I would. Before he left, he kissed me and gave me a last long look.

People come and people go—that's life!

*   *   *

The gentle people of Bali matched my own gentleness. I let the women hold my hand as they were trying to sell me something and was glad when I could make use of what they had to offer.

Often, there was a heartfelt exchange for the good of all of us. It made us all happy. Whenever I felt my heart involved, it went fine. I rarely felt hustled by them like I did in India.

On the beach of Kuta, I watched the surfers and was fascinated by the idea of riding waves. I only had seen windsurfing and had never felt interested in it but this was different. Maybe one day I would give it a try.

On the third day, I received a phone call from Paolo, the man I had met at Good Karma with his daughter. He was horrified that I was staying in *the worst part of town* when he picked me up on his motorbike. He said, "Come, I show you something different!"

He drove me to his home and explained to me that he had just rented a house next door for one of his clients who was arriving a couple of days later. Until then I could stay there if I liked it. I felt a bit uncomfortable and didn't know what to say. Was he just kind to me or was there an obligation involved?

I was honest with him and told him how I was feeling. He assured me there was no duty whatsoever coming along with his offer and showed me the house that was amazing!

"A whole house with two bedrooms, a small one and one to host a king, with an absolutely beautiful bathroom, all to myself?" I felt amazed and accepted my "good karma".

We went to the beach bar of a classy hotel where he and his friends used to hang out. They were all beautiful people and no one seemed to be aware that I hardly knew their friend. Or were they all aware of it and just so used to new people showing up? Were they in general open and welcoming to everyone?

However, we had a good time and stayed for the sunset. Then we went back to the house, or better to the two houses, for a shower before going out again for dinner.

While we were eating we shared parts of the story of our life. He was Spanish and had lived on Bali for many years. He was dealing with Balinese furniture.

We talked a lot about relationships. He had been with a German woman, who also was a yoga teacher, for the last few years and had recently split up with her. She seemed to be similar to me in some ways, often going her own ways and moving independently from him. He on the other hand had many similarities with my Greek partner, needing a woman to be there for him and thinking more in we-and-us-terms.

In a way, we served for each other to reflect on our last partnerships. Listening to the other side, expressed by a neutral person, made it easier to gain more understanding of it. He was a man who liked to give a lot. I could see how he cared for the women in his life; for his daughters—he had another daughter who stayed with the mother at this time—and his different partners. He had a soft heart. Behind his words, I sensed something like a midlife crisis and feelings of being rejected and of not much value anymore. I thought that he deserved to be loved and cared for, too!

I still felt like I was swimming in the honey, most of the times, and I was willing to give him all the love and care he needed at this time. By giving to him, I felt like I was giving something back to my Greek partner, if this makes sense.

What is love?

To me it is not something that you get from another person. It is an energy that we receive from the universe, the source, God—call it as you like—when our heart is open. It fills our chest until it's over flowing; out of our mouth in the form of sweet words and out of our hands in form of nurturing actions. We can give it to anyone we chose to!

I chose to give it to Paolo and he, in return, showed me the beautiful hidden corners of the wider area of Kuta. He took me to a bar where a band played finest world-music and introduced me to good-quality-night-life.

I also felt love pouring out of my heart towards his daughter, who reminded me of my own daughter.

In India, *any* woman that has the age to be our mother is addressed as mother; *any* man that could be our father is called father; *any* person that has the age to be our child is called son or daughter. The same applies to brother and sister. That made me realize: we are all family—a human family—and can treat each other like this!

My stay on Bali ended when my tourist visa ran out. I remember Paolo saying to me: "What do you want to do in New Zealand? There are only cattle and sheep there!"

I knew better!

During the long hours of my flight, I reviewed my journey so far. I thought about the men I had encountered. Some years ago in Greece, I had wished for love and I had wished for freedom. Now I was truly living it.

". . . And hadn't *Free Love* been one of the ideals the hippies had when they wanted to change the world?" I thought to myself. Many of them though—including me in the past—had paid for it with a lot of personal suffering. Few were ready for it. Now, I was finally experiencing it and it felt great! I was away from my partner and we had given each other the freedom for this. There was a risk involved though: we both could find someone new and fall so deeply in love that we would move on into a new partnership. Hadn't I already felt ready for it during my encounter-workshop in Greece?

I remembered how I had felt a wish to experience "deep love" and devoting myself to it. I also had received a message for finding my soul mate in New Zealand. Was he really somewhere out there? . . .

In Rishikesh, I had felt in my soul that this was so. How would I find him?

That would change my life, again, but until then I would enjoy this state of having lovers in freedom.

I felt as if I was filling up with deep gratitude: I was moving around in freedom, following my heart and loving my life!

*   *   *

Landing

I had sometimes fantasized about Jason picking me up from the airport on my arrival in Auckland. Now, it wasn't him picking me up but it was Sarah, the English woman I had become friends with on the airplane, when I flew out of New Zealand.

So, on my second visit I was already welcomed back by a friend!

She took me home and let me rest and get some more sleep in her bed, while she had to return to her work place.

Gratefully, I sank into her bed, glad about her friendly hospitality. When she came back we went out for dinner and talked and talked and talked . . .

She wanted to hear everything about India and she told me about her stay in Thailand. After her father's death, she had taken some time out for herself and stopped over in Thailand on her way back to New Zealand.

Though we were quite tired in the end of the day, we kept on talking even when we had returned to her place and gone to bed. It was like we had been friends for years!

Like two young girls we were giggling, when the conversation took a turn to one of women's favourite subjects: men.

It is a never ending subject too, and it ended for me only, when I was carried away by a sweet, sweet sleep; sweetened by all the memories, the men, I'd been with on my journey, and had left behind.

I spent my first days in Auckland, adjusting to the different life style. Compared to Asia life seemed so organized and structured to me. I didn't like it much and was suffering a culture shock.

The weather didn't help either, as it was much cooler: partly sunny, partly rainy, windy and cloudy. The people were much "cooler" too; in both ways: being cool was cool and people lived more from their head than heart.

Not everybody was as warm and welcoming as my friend Sarah who was sharing the house with two other flatmates.

Sarah left the house early in the morning, worked all day in an office and came back in the late afternoon.

I spent my time exploring the city and started to write down my travel experiences so far. It was early December and I thought, the best Christmas present that I could give to my family, was sharing my journey with them.

The evenings, when Sarah was home, were always communicative and giggly.

She told me about a beautiful beach. It was the place she used to escape to, when she wanted to get away from the city. A friend of hers lived there and she sometimes stayed at his place, when he needed to be away for work.

She went on telling me about her friend and how skilful he was with his hands. She told me how he had done so much work on the place, he was renting, transforming it into a place of beauty.

She said that there was a time, when she nearly had got together with him. Then, she had met the love of her life and he, too, had got together with another woman and had married her. His marriage didn't last though and he was living on his own again.

She suggested visiting the beach and her friend on the weekend, and I liked the idea. I was curious to meet the man, who lived by himself on a hill not far from a wild West Coast beach. "Could this be a man for me?" I heard myself thinking.

The drive out there took us forty-five minutes. At first, I got bored with the motorway and the suburb-like areas, we passed, but then we drove into a beautiful valley. The road passed a stunning rocky wall and went along a mixture of farmland, paddocks and native bush.

Her friend's place was not as deserted, as I had imagined it. The road that led to it had actually many dwellings to its right and left side.

When we got to the house, we found her friend in front of his computer, playing around on Google earth. We joined him and I showed Sarah, where I lived in Greece. I was amazed to suddenly see the house that had been my home for the last years.

Nearly four months had passed, since the day I had left.

Her friend, whose name was Steve, offered us a glass of wine and showed us around his garden. In there, on top of the hill, was another little cottage that his landlady kept as a holiday home.

He opened it for us, so we could have a look inside. When he lifted the blinds, it gave us a view down the valley to the ocean. I immediately thought, that this would be the ideal place to retreat for writing.

When Steve saw that we liked it in the little cottage, he went and brought the wine and some cheese up there. As we sat around the table, talking and enjoying the view, the wine and the cheese, I suddenly remembered the moment when I was in Kashmir on a boat with the Frenchman, both of us dreaming about red wine—"rouge"—and cheese!

So here I was, enjoying exactly that! "Thanks, universe!"

Later, I convinced Sarah to go for a walk on the beach. She wasn't too keen as the weather was windy and overcast but she finally agreed to do it.

Steve said he would wait at the house for us to come back and then take us to a Japanese Restaurant for dinner.

When we arrived at the beach, we got to feel the power of the elements. The wind nearly blew us away. It was so strong. The ocean was wild too. The surf was roaring and crashing against the rocks. We needed to scream at each other to be heard, what made us laugh out loud.

I saw some rocks, covered with something black. When I went closer, I saw that it was full of tiny, black, beautifully shining mussels. There was a large cave at the end of the beach. The tide was out and we were able to enter it. The inside reminded me somehow of a cathedral and filled me with awe.

"What a magical powerful place!" I said. I was glad that we had come here.

"I thought, you would like it", Sarah smiled amusedly.

Quite euphoric we got back to the house and found Steve ready to go. We followed him in Sarah's car into the next town and joined him into a small, minimally but harmonically decorated, restaurant.

I had never been in a Japanese Restaurant before and wasn't quite sure what to choose. The Japanese people on the table next to ours had something that looked beautiful and tasty. I asked the waitress what they were having and she answered that it was the platter for two persons. Steve immediately said that he would share it with me and a little later I sat next to him, a man I hardly knew, sharing a meal with him.

Sarah watched us from the opposite side of the table and seemed once again amused. When we said goodbye to him, I kissed him on the cheek and he looked, as if he'd woken up after a long psychic sleep.

"Who knows, maybe I'll see you again", I said.

The next day, Sarah's flatmate had a go at me because I had by mistake used one of his avocados. He said, it was ok—he just wanted me to be aware!

Still, the tone of his voice made me feel "not ok" and uncomfortable.

In the evening, Sarah got a phone call and I heard her spelling my name, as she was talking on the phone to someone. When she came back into her room, she said that Steve had just phoned and had offered us the little cottage for a stay. He had said that it was empty most of the times and we would be welcome to use it, if we wanted.

I looked at her and realized that I wanted indeed!

I was happy to get away from the nasty flatmate and have a place where I could be by myself and focus on writing.

I rang Steve back and he picked me up the next day. Who would have thought that only a day later, I would find myself back in the little cottage by the beach, relieved from the tension that I had felt around Sarah's flatmate and stoked to be in the ideal place for writing my story?

In return for my stay, I offered Steve to massage him.

Once again, I sat down at the table with the view over the valley down to the ocean. 'How did I get so lucky, again?'

I started writing right after my early morning mantra chanting. I had my morning cuppa, while I went on writing. I had some breakfast, when I needed a break and went on writing. I went for a shower, when I needed the next break and went on writing. Like this it went on all day. I interrupted my writing only to look after my body's needs.

Nobody was there to distract or disturb me, which was great.

In the evening, when Steve came home from work, I massaged him. I went early to bed and got up early the next day, just to follow the same routine.

The next night, I stayed a little longer at Steve's and we had a look at the photos from my travels on his large TV screen. He started to tell me more about his life and his travels.

Slowly, we got to know each other during the evenings of those days.

When he was invited by one of his friends for dinner, I simply was invited along. We kept the massage short that night. When we arrived at the farm of his friend's family, I saw that we were not the only guests. I got to meet some more of his friends.

They all had known each other for many years and revealed to me some of the stories of their mutual past. They were all very welcoming and friendly to me—the newcomer and foreigner—and I felt embraced by their open and humorous ways. They asked me about my Christmas plans and when I said, I didn't have any, invited me to their farm for lunch on Christmas' Day.

"How nice of them", I thought. "Or were they thinking of Steve and trying to find some company for him?"

I thanked them for the invitation and said that I didn't know yet where I would be by then.

I really didn't know! After finishing my travel story for my family, I wanted to go on a tour to the far north of New Zealand, where I hadn't been yet. In the travel guide it said that there was one of the world's ten best diving spots by the Poor Knights Islands.

Still, my story wasn't finished yet. Originally, I thought, it would take me two or three full days of writing. Now, it looked as if I needed at least two more days. I asked Steve if I could stay a little longer. He thought, it should be alright, as his land lady usually phones him when she wants to come out for the weekend. "Otherwise we'll have a surprise" he said jokingly.

When "the surprise" really happened, he was still at work. I was fully absorbed in my writing and hadn't noticed the arrival of some people at the gate. I only became aware of it, when I suddenly heard a voice right outside the entrance door. Then a knocking followed. I got up to see who was there and in the doorway stood the "surprised" landlady. She had spontaneously come out with some friends to show them her place and was obviously not expecting anyone to stay in there.

What could be done here? I apologized to her and as quickly as I could I packed all my stuff together. Within minutes I had cleared the space. So she could welcome her guests without any signs of someone else staying there.

Luckily, I found the backdoor to Steve's house open and went inside. When he came home he already knew, what had happened. His landlady had phoned him at work and he too had to apologize to her.

"Well, you better stay with me then" he said jokingly. Tired he let himself fall into an armchair.

"Are you ok?" he asked me with concern.

"Yes. I think, nothing really bad has happened. You're landlady didn't kill me, when she found me in her cottage." I tried to be funny.

"I didn't even have to hang around outside! What about you?"

"I'm ok—just a bit tired."

"What about having a massage and relax?" I suggested. He accepted and when we finished with the massage, his landlady rang again. She was ready to go back into town and said that I could move back into the cottage! So it all ended well.

I noticed, how the experiences of my travels had changed my perspective on things. I had survived the Himalayasandcomparedtothattheincidentseemedrather small. It might have been a little unpleasant—yes—but no one had suffered a big loss.

I thought how the "small tragedies" of everyday life are only significant until a major tragedy happens. Then they suddenly become so relatively unimportant!

How often do we forget this and spend hours of our life judging ourselves and others for our behaviour when we just quickly could get over it and on to the next living experience?

*　　*　　*

The following day, I finished writing down my travel experiences for my family. I had once again lived through my journey so far and felt a lot of gratitude for all that I had experienced. I also felt gratitude that I had the ability to go on such a journey. True, I had given up my house for it, which was very painful. The freedom to fly around the planet had had its price. Still, my life was so enriched by all the experiences.

"What else is possible?" I wondered. What else was waiting around the corner that I couldn't see yet but that I soon would encounter on this journey?

Steve had considered to take me in his van around Northland but had finally decided not to go on a tour before Christmas. He had work to do around the house, he said.

He invited Sarah and me to a party at his place on Christmas Eve and suggested to do another tour together in his van after Christmas.

"That sounds good!" I said. I also wanted to explore the Coromandel Peninsula and the region around the East Cape and liked the idea to do it with him.

"And I'll talk to Sarah about the party."

On my last day, he had offered to give me a massage and to my own surprise I agreed to it. It occasionally happens that I receive a massage offer by a male client that I always decline, not taking a risk it may hide a sexual approach.

On our drive out here, Steve had told me that when he was still at school, one of his teachers had taught them how to massage each other and how he had enjoyed that. That's why his offer seemed innocent enough to me and I thought he had learned some techniques. The massage lesson had been a long time ago though! His hands felt nervous and unsure. Patiently, I let him find his rhythm into it and though he didn't know any techniques my body relaxed under his hands. His massage went on and on and I realized that he couldn't take his hands off me. After two hours, he himself realized that this couldn't go on forever and stopped.

When I had dressed and had the obligatory glass of water, he had stretched out on the floor.

"You know" he said "you can also stay in this house. It's big enough. My bed is big enough. Sarah has stayed there with me before."

My answer was, "That would be dangerous!" and he agreed. "I feel very attracted to you", he finally admitted.

By then, I was aware of that. What should I do with it? He looked so open and vulnerable that it somehow moved me. The air between us felt charged. I better leave now. Tomorrow he would give me a lift to the bus stop in town from where I would travel up north. I said goodnight and retreated into the small cottage.

For a while, I sat outside gazing at the millions of stars on the clear night-sky. I once again felt so beautifully free and adventurous. Once again, I thought how my life had become this beautiful adventure, as it continued to unfold in wonderful ways.

I remembered the time seven years ago, when I had felt that I couldn't breathe in my own house. That was what I had longed for when I left my house and partner. I had not felt ready to settle, then. I had felt so thirsty for adventures and the man hadn't been the right one for me either.

Now, I was meeting so many beautiful people but no one could *have* me!

The next day, I packed my things together. This time, I could take my time for it, while Steve was doing some work in his garden. When we were both ready, he drove me into town.

"Hey, you have a partner in Greece" he said. "If I had thought about that, I wouldn't have said what I was saying last night."

"It's okay" I replied. "You know, when you said it, I suddenly felt the same but I couldn't tell you this last night."

We both knew that this would have led to consequences!

Not that I was worried about my partner in Greece. It was Sarah, who I was concerned about. She had once mentioned that she, at some point, nearly got together with Steve. I wasn't sure about her feelings for him and I didn't want to mess up our friendship for another erotic adventure of mine!

*　　*　　*

On the bus to Whangarei I switched on my cell phone. It had been switched off all these days because the beach had no cell phone coverage. I had left a sign with my phone number in some of the Backpacker's hostels in Auckland, saying that I was looking for a lift to the far north, up to Cape Reinga. Someone had replied to it. I contacted the person, who was still keen to go.

We arranged to meet in Whangarei the next day, and continue the trip from there together.

I was excited to go diving again. It would be my first dive after the diving course and in totally different water. Nothing was arranged yet and I used the time on the bus to check where I would stay. I chose a backpacker's hostel that offered a pick-up from the bus and learned that they also did the booking for the diving excursion. Did it get any easier than that? Everything went with effortless flow.

Steve had been very helpful and supportive to get my handwritten story copied and posted and my Christmas present for my family was now on its way to them. Would it be of any interest to them?

My mother and daughter would most likely soak it up. About my father and brother I wasn't too sure. It didn't include my erotic adventures. In thought of the relationship between my family and my Greek partner, I had left this part out. They might not understand and didn't need to know, I decided. Surprised, I noticed that I was somehow missing Steve. I had become used to him being around in these last days.

Early the next morning, I was picked-up by a shuttle bus to the diving centre. Another girl and myself were the only persons on the large bus. The diving centre was very busy though. I was taken out to the Poor Knights Islands by boat with a large group of divers. The ride was quite rough and I started to feel a little sick. When we arrived at the islands, the water was calm. A subtropical current from the Coral Sea had arrived, making it so special for diving, as it brought lots of colourful tropical fish with it. The water temperature was not tropical though. Compared to Bali it was shocking cold. Its clarity made up for it.

Soon I was amazed by the magical site and had forgotten about the cold water. Manta rays were emerging from an underwater forest and little colourful fish attacked my finger as I came too close to their breeding spot. It didn't hurt and was very funny.

Back on board, we had a hot shower to warm us up. The atmosphere was now uplifted. Everybody had enjoyed a wonderful dive and people were more engaged talking to each other.

As we drove back to shore, dolphins showed up beside our boat. The boat dropped its speed and we could watch them swimming along next to us. How could it get any better than this? Once again, I felt blessed by the experience.

Tired but very, very happy I got back to the hostel. The guy who was going to give me a lift around Northland had also arrived, and we started planning and preparing our trip for the next day. He was German from Arabic descend and seemed nice. Again, one event kept flowing into the next. It was great!

He had the car and I had some music for our tour through the pristine, beautiful countryside. He drove so fast that it rather felt like flying than driving. Before I could worry, he told me that he used to drive an ambulance as a job.

We visited a magnificent waterfall, a glowworm cave and drove all the way up through the Bay of Islands to the far tip of the North Island, where the Pacific Ocean meets the Tasman Sea.

One can watch the two oceans coming together at this point. Absorbed into the sight of this play, I was facing my own feelings. Feelings for Jason that I had pushed away, surfaced once again. I realized that I couldn't just visit him and his new partner. I still held a wish within my heart to be close to him and hold him in my arms. There was nothing I could do but witness my feelings, accept them and *do nothing* despite them.

To the Maoris, Cape Reinga is the gateway through which the souls leave the land and travel into the spirit world. What was it that Jason had touched in me that my own soul was longing for so strongly? Was now the time, to let that part of me move on too?

Holding this question in my heart, I went very quiet for the rest of our trip. The evening sky was stunning that night. Purple, orange and golden clouds covered the sky. To me, they were reflecting one wish, one calling. "Jason!" they were calling.

We spend the night in a campground that had cottages and dormitories. Most guests were surfers.

I started bleeding. The menstrual blood seemed to flow right out of my heart.

The next day, the unfulfilled longing had turned into hurt. I felt sorry for my travel mate because I probably wasn't much fun to be with, that day. I was suffering silently as we drove through the beautiful country. We had now reached the Kauri Forest. I lay my heart down at the feet of the magnificent *Lord of the Forest* Tane Mahuta, one of the largest Kauri Trees in New Zealand. The majestic power of the tree gave me some comfort and relief. As we drove on, my heart felt much lighter.

We reached Auckland that night and I once again found shelter in Sarah's room and in her company. She was moving out and I had promised to help her move.

For one more day, we had her room to stay in. It was quite late when I arrived and we were both tired. Soon though, we had both cheered up in each other's company and I had to tell her everything about the trip and my stay at Steve's.

I told her that it had got a little hot between us on my last night. She laughed and was not surprised. She said she had already seen something between Steve and me when we shared our meal in the Japanese Restaurant.

She assured me that she was absolutely fine with whatever turn that would take. I told her that we were both invited to a party at his place on Christmas Eve. I explained that it felt right to me to spend Christmas Eve with the two people that were closest to me in this country, where I was a foreigner. I realized further that to me Steve's place felt mostly like *home* here. She could understand that and agreed.

A great change was happening in her life, too. She had been inspired by me, taking my freedom to living my dream and the glow that I had arrived with from my travels in India and Bali. She told me, that when she first saw me at the airport, she had thought: "Whatever it is, she has, I want it!"

Now, she was quitting her office job, moving her things into storage to house-sit for a while, before she would go on a journey to England and India.

The next day, I helped her to pack her things into containers. Steve and another friend of hers came to help load it all into two vans and into storage. I naturally ended up in Steve's van, when we were moving her things. He asked me if we would come to his party. He smiled, when I said that I had spoken to Sarah and she had agreed.

After the job was done, Sarah treated us to lunch and coffee. Then, the two men went about their own business and Sarah and I went to the house, she was going to look after for the next weeks.

It was a sunny afternoon when we drove out to Steve's place for the party. We would stay there overnight. Sarah was going to drive back into town on Christmas Day, while I was going to join Steve for lunch at his friends' farm.

When we arrived a small crowd of friends and neighbours were already there. Everyone had contributed a plate and I added mine. The atmosphere was joyful and relaxed. People knew each other well and they had a happy catch up.

Sarah and me were new to them and of course I was asked, where I was from. When I said that I lived in Greece, they told me that they had a friend who'd lived in Greece. At first I didn't click, but as they went into more details about him and his life, I realized that it was my friend they were talking about!

I couldn't believe it! What a coincidence! Here I was amongst the friends of the man, whom I had once fallen in love with! Back then, this friend had spoken about a beach where he used to go surfing. So *this* was the beach, he had spoken about!

I remembered how I had dreamed about being there together with him. And here I was—not with him—but life still had taken me to the, back then, unknown place of my dreams! It was hard to believe!

Steve was busy, filling everyone's glasses with a fruity summer-punch. His ex-wife was also there. She sat down next to Sarah and me and pointed out to us, that is was her, who had planted all the flowers in the garden. Her and Steve had separated more than a year ago but she still used to come around for visits. They were still good friends.

Some of Steve's friends seemed surprised though to see her there.

When the music became livelier, the three of us got up and danced together. One of the many guys around, who was already quite drunk walked up to us, looked at us and said, "You can all have me!—Any of the three of you can have me, if you like!" He smiled at us but—"no thank you"—we were not interested.

He was still around after everyone else had left, playing songs on his guitar to Sarah and me, until Steve made him understand that it was time for him to go home. It was late and we were all looking forward to getting some rest.

Tired we went inside. Sarah sank into an armchair and I rested on the floor. Steve kindly let us stay in his bedroom and offered to sleep on the couch. He was still busy, tidying a few things up. When Sarah went to the bathroom, I suddenly felt his arms around me.

I wasn't surprised though I hadn't expected it either. I hadn't thought about what could happen, might happen or would happen. I basically hadn't thought.

When he held me from behind, it felt just natural. I turned around to look at him and he kissed me.

This was when we both got a surprise! We were both surprised *how* good it felt kissing each other! Call it chemistry, call it magnetism—it carried us away, closer and closer. Luckily, Sarah never came back from the bathroom! Later, I quietly slipped into the bed next to her.

On our way to the farm Steve said, "Hey, we have a little secret now."

"Yes", I smiled, noticing that he wanted no one to know what had happened last night. I was fine with that. I was already looking forward to the coming night when we would have the house to ourselves.

My head was feeling slightly heavy from the fruit punch. At the farm we were welcomed with more alcohol. I had to ask for an aspirin to be able to enjoy the Christmas meal in English tradition.

We sat outside on the veranda looking into a beautiful flowery summer garden. It couldn't be more different from Christmas in Europe!

When we finally returned to the house, everything turned out to be totally different from what I had imagined.

Instead of the blissful chemistry I had enjoyed the night before, my body had to deal with the chemistry of the painkiller and the alcohol. It obviously didn't like it and instead of stretching out in bed, I found myself stretched out on the floor, feeling dizzy and shaky.

What was right about that that I wasn't getting? Was that cosmic humour at play?

*   *   *

The next day, we left for our tour. We had decided to finally go around the East Cape, as the Coromandel region gets extremely busy during the Christmas season. Steve had arranged to visit some of his friends at Whakatane in the Bay of Plenty.

We spent the first night at their house. The following day, they took us to a batch in a beautiful bay where they were going to have a holiday. We didn't stay long. We had a coffee with them and went on our way, exploring the remote area around the East Cape. The region is known for its remoteness and Maori culture. Just driving through it, we didn't get to see much of the Maori culture but definitely enjoyed its remoteness.

We stayed in the van by a beach and watched the sun rising out of the ocean. Just for Steve I repeated the swim in my sea-through underwear. I had told him the story of my ocean appearance after swimming with the dolphins and he had asked for a repetition.

"Just like in a movie" was his comment, when I came slowly out of the water and kissed him.

I thought that this is the first sunrise of the new day, due to the International dateline. "Where time starts" was a line of a Greek song, I had listened to on my way to New Zealand. The song went: "I travel with you into your open soul, on a road without return, . . . I want to reach the edge of the world, where time starts . . ."

I had been singing this song all the way along. Now I was amazed, how it had fulfilled itself!

"On a road without return . . . ? Would that also be the case?", I thought to myself.

Traveling on a round-the-world—ticket meant definitely that I kept moving forward in one direction. Was there any other meaning to it?

When we left the beach behind us, Steve said, "I can give you anything!" and I said, "I can give you myself", as I had nothing else to give.

* * *

Our tour ended in Napier. Once again, he took me to the bus stop. From there I would get on a bus to Wellington and Steve would drive back to his home. Our goodbye was quick and unspectacular.

This time, we were sure that we would see each other again at some stage. I had left a bag with some of my stuff at his place. I was going to spend some time as a willing worker at the Hostel Shambhala and wanted to visit a Yoga Retreat on the way there. I didn't know, how long exactly I would be in the South Island.

In Wellington, I would meet up with Daniela and Sarah. We had arranged to celebrate New Year's Eve together. I was looking forward to the reunion of the three women, who had become friends on an airplane nine months earlier; the "three witches", as we had called ourselves. We were all involved in healing and had some psychic abilities.

As I got closer to Wellington, I couldn't help myself—I started thinking of Jason. He and Wellington, to me had become one and the same.

It seemed wrong not to see him at all. I just *had* to see him. Best thing was to meet him somewhere neutral for a coffee, I decided. I sent him a text and—yes—he agreed.

The bus arrived, while Daniela was still at work. I had some time ahead of me before she would pick me up. A cold wind was blowing, as is so typical for this city.

I walked along the waterfront and couldn't get warm. I started to feel a little bit lost and unprotected. On my first visit to Wellington, I had felt the same before meeting Jason. Would Wellington always welcome me like this?

Later, I found myself embraced by Daniela's Balkan temperament, which reminded me a lot of Greece. This was our first time together since the plane trip, and I got to know her a little better before Sarah arrived.

The first appointment with Jason fell through, because his partner had got the flu and he had to look after her. If it hadn't been for the companionship of the two ladies, I could have felt quite terrible. They both liked to hear about my *new* romance with Steve. That made me aware that I too had moved on. It was just right to once and forever let go of all the passion, hopes and dreams, connected to Jason.

As we were talking about Steve and me, Sarah suddenly had a vision of me in a wedding dress. I felt my womb tingling. It was then, when I became aware of a deeper, inner knowing that I had met the man, I was to marry.

How well it was arranged by the universe, that only after I had realized this, I got to meet Jason. We had a lovely afternoon in a cafe in a park. We both enjoyed sitting in each other's company and energy and the magnetic spark was still there. Nothing needed to follow that. The good feeling was the soothing gift I took away with me from the short time we spent together and all was good. I was finally in peace with it.

*   *   *

From Wellington I flew to Nelson. The three "witches" had got some magic working for each other and felt we were all in a better place.

"When and where would we meet next time?" I was wondering, as I looked at the ocean from above. The Marlborough Sounds, with the play of water and land, looked so beautiful.

On my first visit to New Zealand, I had enjoyed my stay in Nelson with its artistic flair. Now, I was hoping for some live music events or even just some street music or theatre. I hitchhiked into town and got a lift from one of the passengers, who had been on the same aircraft with me. I asked him if there were any music events happening in Nelson, but he had been away for two weeks and didn't know.

Feeling a little tired, I checked into a backpacker's hostel, right in the centre of town and lay down on my bed. Maybe I would be able to have a short nap, before exploring what was happening in town.

As I was trying to sleep, I heard music. It sounded really good. So I got up to identify the source of it. A band was playing in the street right next to the hostel!

Quickly, I got up and went down. That was exactly what I had hoped for, and it got even better: I learned that it was the first day of Nelson's annual Jazz Fest!

I felt so lucky and smiled as I sat there, enjoying the music. When they were playing "You make me feel like natural woman", I suddenly thought of Steve.

Spontaneously, I phoned him to share my joy with him. Instead of him I got the answer machine on the phone and left a message, saying: "Hey, listen to the streets of Nelson! It's awesome here! They have a jazz festival going on here" and before I knew, what I was saying: "Would you like to come down here?" had popped out of my mouth.

The next day—exactly twenty-four hours later—he was there!

"I'm glad I didn't catch your call, because I would have answered: No. I've got work to do!" he said. Then he smiled, "but as I was lying in my hammock with a beer in my hand, I thought to myself, why not? The work can wait!"

So, there we were together again—so much sooner than we both had expected! He had booked his return flight in a week's time, which gave us a whole week together. I had to tell him, that I was going to a yoga retreat after three days and he said not to worry and just do everything as I had planned.

We spent three lovely days in Nelson, enjoying all the music events in parks, pubs and cafes. His brother came over from Blenheim for an afternoon. He was the first member of Steve's family I got to meet.

Steve had rented a car and together we drove to Golden Bay. I had informed the yoga centre that I was traveling with a friend and they were ok with him coming along. When we drove up the dirt road to the retreat Anahata, he had no idea what to expect and felt a little nervous. I appreciated that he *dared* to come along. In order to "have it nice" we had booked the Luxury Yurt for our accommodation.

On our first day, he left the spacious, beautifully rounded building only for the provided meals. Just being in the ashram-like environment was enough for a start.

The next day I had my private session with Swami Muktidharma, who was the main teacher there.

Talking to him and being blessed by his wisdom, it became quite clear to me that for the spiritual guidance that I was seeking, more time was required. Still, the talk had been inspiring and left me charged with energy.

When the Swami gave a talk to the whole group, Steve came along and received his first introduction into yoga. From then on, he participated in all the classes of the program. For me it was the first time that a man was with me during a retreat. None of my former partners had ever followed me into a yoga centre and I was very pleased with the situation. When we left, we both felt very good.

Next destination was the backpacker's hostel Shambhala, where I would start my job as a willing worker. The owner John didn't want me to start right away. He said, I could take it easy for as long as my friend was there and just have a holiday.

So we had time to explore the region, visit the Pupu Springs, Farewell Spit and Wharariki Beach. It was glorious!

We stayed in one of the double bedrooms with a large window that looked right over the bush out to the ocean. The room we'd got was next to the room, where I had stayed on my first visit. It was simple, but harmoniously beautiful, with some artwork on the walls. I loved its peaceful atmosphere and cosiness. I also loved to be there with Steve. Before Steve left, he told me that he loved me.

*   *   *

After he had left, I moved into a tent in the forest that was there for woofers to stay, and started my job as a willing worker.

It was now my job to look after the rooms I had stayed in before, keep them clean and tidy and change the bed sheets. Of course I had to clean the rest of the rooms too, as well as all the other facilities, but I was not the only woofer there. There were four of us from different countries of the world.

Once again, I was in an international place and loved the diversity of it. Many of the guests were seekers and on their own personal journey of discovery and self-discovery. We had many stories and experiences to tell and share. We also had many questions to ask; questions where to go in New Zealand and questions where to go in life.

For the moment, we had come together in an auspicious place: Shambhala, according to an ancient Tibetan Buddhist myth, the "Hidden Paradise".

Most of us were aware that this place was inside us and that the inner journey through meditation could one day lead us there. Still, the grounds of the hostel Shambhala, its many artistic little corners and niches were momentarily the outer paradise, we were enjoying. It was a reflection of what we could find inside us: peace and beauty.

Not everyone perceived it in this way. To some people it was just a hostel; with corners of imperfection maybe. To others it was so boring, that they left right away. To many of us though it had become a hidden paradise.

The jewel of it was the large meditation hall that was also used for hatha yoga. Here, I could do my own daily practice and join the yoga class that was offered twice weekly by a neighbouring practitioner.

Other hours were reserved for meditation only. There were guided meditations by the owner, who was the embodiment of equanimity. He seemed like a walking-talking meditation, as he was wandering around the place, always busy and alert—and always relaxed.

I felt grateful to be and work in such a place. Soon I was offering sessions to our guests; massage, craniosacral therapy and Reiki. I also started to teach some yoga in the mornings.

In the afternoons, I was enjoying the privacy of my tent in the forest; relaxing, drinking tea and reading a book. This was the time of the day, when the sun got there and made it friendly and warm. On rainy or cloudy days, I stayed inside the tent. On sunny days, I pulled the mattress into the sunshine and let it tan my skin.

The birds, especially the little fantails, often came really close to me. I loved their company. They were the pleasant inhabitants of the forest. Rather unpleasant were the possums that came out at night time.

One night, I woke up and felt the presence of another being with me. I didn't know what it was and my heart started racing. Then I became aware, that a possum had invited itself into my tent. The tent had no zip, but straps along its entrance. It was pitch dark and I couldn't see it. I started to make a lot of noises to scare it away but it obviously wasn't impressed much. Wherever it was, it just kept still. Then I heard some rustling and it finally left.

That was the start of a series of possum dreams that filled my nights and sleeping hours from now on. The owner of the hostel had set up a cage-like trap that would keep it alive. I was dreaming of different versions of catching and dealing to the possum. The afternoon rest had become essential to me, as the nights didn't guarantee a good night's sleep. Sometimes, two possums were fighting with each other right outside of my tent. I had found a way to keep it closed, so no possum could come inside. Other than that, I just had to get used to them. They were sometimes scary—yes—but at least they were not dangerous.

Some nights, I slept deep and well, though. These were the ones after a visit to the Mussel Inn, a near by café. It is well known for its live-music-events and its choice of naturally brewed beers and ciders.

A colourful crowd used to come together for those events. Sometimes, people were seated and just listening to a concert, but more often people would get up and dance. Tables often needed to be carried outside to make room for the dancers.

All my life I had enjoyed dancing. The combination of a small amount of the healthy beer and good sound could transport me instantly into a "higher-vibration-state". I felt my whole being uplifted by it and every cell of my body singing and dancing. This would be the moment, where I would get up and let my body dance. When it did, it was better that I didn't interfere or get in the way of it. The best was, when I just let my body do its thing!

In my life there are times for meditation and times to party. It was terrific that here, I was having both! I felt beautifully in balance!

*   *   *

While I was in Shambhala, Steve and me kept in contact through our cell phones. Every morning, we would send a sweet good-morning-message to each other and occasionally we would talk. The distance made us aware of how much we were already connected.

On Valentine's Day it was raining heavily. One of the other woofers and I drove into town. We found shelter in a cafe and made ourselves comfortable in the sitting area with two soft couches. Someone was playing love songs on the piano. I hadn't heard a word from Steve on that day. He was on a hike with his best friend and out of cell phone range.

"How was that for a sign, Valentine's and no word from my honey?", I thought to myself. Then something neat happened; as I leaned back into the couch, I felt something at my backside. I looked, what it was, and found a small chocolate heart in pink foil.

Was this the universe telling me that romantic love was there for me? I took it as a sign and smiled.

One evening, I received a message from him, saying that he loved my smile and that he loved being with me. I wrote back, "And I love you!"

It was time to see each other again!

I took a one-week-break from my woofing job and flew up to Auckland.

Our being together had a new intensity and closeness. He had told all his friends and regular visitors to stay away for a week. During this week in the privacy of his home, our being together deepened to the bliss of love.

One evening, after a walk to the ocean, we looked into each other's eyes and knew; we had found each other!

*   *   *

Back in Shambhala, I realized that he—Steve—had finally got me and my dreams showed me the reality of having two men now. My feelings for my partner in Greece hadn't changed. I just knew now that I had found the man that was my destiny.

I would have to write a letter to my partner in Greece!

Sitting by the ocean, I thought about my life and which turn it would take. I could extend my tourist visa from three to six months. Due to the law of immigration, I then had to stay six months out of the country, before I could return as a tourist. I could see this happening, living half the year in New Zealand, spending the other half working in Greece and also travel through different other countries. India, as the home of yoga, would be my third main destination.

I loved the idea. That just looked like the life of my dreams to me! I felt filled with deep gratitude for how everything had developed. Had I found what I was looking for? Yes—and more!

I realized *I was* on a journey to the most beautiful places on earth. I *was* traveling from one paradise to the next. I felt, I *had* found the deep love, I had been longing for.

I felt, I had finally fallen in love with life on earth, with *my life on earth!*

*   *   *

When autumn came, I left the hostel and returned to Auckland, to the beach and to Steve. We wanted to spend the rest of my time in New Zealand together and find out how we would get along with each other in daily life. He was so used to living alone. How would it be for him to have me around day and night? I was so used to following my own inner voice, and doing what ever I sensed was right at any time. Could that work?

I wrote to one of my friends that I was going to stay with Steve now to "live love". She responded how beautiful that sounded: *live love!* By now that was what it had come down to in every aspect, in my relationship with him, and in my life in general.

A song popped into my mind that goes: "Now that we found love what are we going to do with it?"—a question to ask every single day or even every single moment.

To me it was *being it*, being *with* it and treating each other nicely!

During the next two months, we had plenty of opportunity for practicing that. Steve had to work on some days, but most of the time he was at home and we could be together, as if the universe had made us a little gift.

We were blessed with time to go for walks, time to have long conversations and time to make love. It felt like an extended honeymoon. It was *Heaven on Earth*!

Was this real? It seemed like such a dream. Would I wake up from it one day or was this a possibility of how life could be?

There was no effort in our living together. There seemed to be a natural harmony. We were doing little jobs around the house and garden and when we felt it was enough, we were just chilling in the two hammocks with an ice-cold beer.

I enjoyed that we did all the housework and the cooking together. That was one thing that I had missed with my Greek partner! I really liked, that in New Zealand it was *normal* for men to cook and wash dishes.

When I watched Steve looking after his animals and his garden with so much care, I knew that this was the way he would look after me too.

I remembered the encounter-workshop that I had done a year ago and the way, I had channelled the different energies of having my needs fulfilled or not. Chances looked good, that in his garden I would bloom too.

* * *

My journey wasn't over yet. Soon I would leave for Fiji and California. Sarah would come to Fiji with me. There, we would have a holiday together. Some adventures were still lying ahead of me, before I would return to Europe. For six months I had to stay out of New Zealand now.

What would happen with Steve and me? When would we see each other again?

Steve looked at me. We were standing on the veranda in front of the little cottage, holding each other.

"I want to make you a gift" he said.

"Please take my gift!" In his voice was a tremble.

"What was coming now?" I wondered.

"My gift, is a retreat at the Satyananda Yoga Ashram in India! I want to go there and it might change my life. I want you to be with me then!"

Wow—I felt speechless. That truly was a big gift! Could I take it? How should I respond?

In my heart, I felt that I wanted nothing more than be with him there. I felt awe for his generosity. His eyes were still fixed on me and looked almost anxious.

"Yes, I take it!" I whispered.

*　　*　　*

We made a plan to meet up in England. Steve wanted to have a holiday there and visit some old friends. When he was in his twenties, he lived and worked in a small town in the south of England and he still used to go back there for holidays.

I would sort out things in Greece and spend a couple of months there, working and earning the money for the next trip. The retreat was his gift for me, but I still needed to pay for the journey. And we had quite a journey planned! We would spend five days in England together and really take this time just to be with each other again, after four months of separation. From England we would travel to India and spend three weeks in Rishikesh, adjusting and adapting to the different culture. There we also would take up a softer yoga routine, before we would go on the retreat in Bihar. After the retreat we would go to Thailand for a holiday, and finally return to New Zealand together.

At some stage in the future, our partnership would allow me to become a resident in New Zealand. Now, I could finally *see* the bridge into my "new life". I somehow had known that through a marriage I would enter the new country. Now, it was really happening and it was so exciting!

I remembered how insecure and shaky I had felt in the beginning, when I first felt "a calling" into something new: a new experience, a new life in a new country.

Of course, it is not necessary to move into a different country in order to make a life change and have a different life experience. For me though, it was right.

In a new place, people don't know us and are open to find out who we are. This makes it possible for us to try out being someone different. Our family and friends already have a picture of who we are. They keep projecting this picture on us, which gives us little freedom to be different. How often do we act in a certain way, just because our friends expect us to behave in that way? This is what keeps us stuck in the same old pattern, even if we in ourselves have already made a step towards change.

Different countries also have different ways of living and doing things. Learning those different ways was the main reason why I had always liked to stay in a different country.

I remembered how I had felt so "alone in the darkness", when I first left my home in the middle of winter and drove all the way up to Northern Greece to encounter my "Self" during the weekend workshop and gain clarity. I remembered how thin my voice had been at the airport, just before my first trip to New Zealand!

Now, I felt so glad I dared and did it! What had I shouted after my bungy jump? I did it, I did it, I did it!

Without taking a risk, would there be an adventure???

The next adventure was soon to start. A couple of days more and I once again would hop on an airplane and discover a different culture.

Once again, I would explore new roads on my journey around the planet.

*   *   *

Steve and I were in the living room of his house. I was playing around with my camera, in an attempt to get him in there and take him with me. I knew he'd be in my heart and in my heart I would take him with me. Still, I wanted to look at him and listen to his voice.

He was moving around the house, feeling a bit uncomfortable with me filming him until I said softly, "Please . . . look at me . . . talk to me!"

"Alright then" he said and settled down on the floor in front of me. He finally looked at me and smiled. His voice became soft.

" . . . You know . . . I'm very happy . . . walking around with a big smile . . . I'm a pretty happy guy anyway but—you made me very happy! . . . And I'm looking forward to the next part!"

I smiled back at him. "This part is still pretty good!"

*   *   *